I0668277

If These Shoes Could Talk

THE AWAKENING

A novel by Jahzara The Savvy Diva

If These Shoes Could Talk © 2014
A novel by Jahzara The Savvy Diva

This novel is a work of fiction. Any resemblance to real people, living or dead, actual events, establishments, organizations, and locales are intended to give the fiction a sense of reality and authenticity. Other names, characters, places, and incidents are either products of the author's imagination or are used fictitiously, as are those fictionalized events and incidents that involve real people and did not occur or are set in the future.
Copyright © 2014 Jahzara, The Savvy Diva
Published by JAHPHUT
P.O. Box 2540 Washington, DC 20013
www.jahphut.com

ISBN: 0977063011
ISBN-13: 9780977063017
LCCN: 2014945001
Written by Jahzara, the Savvy Diva, edited by Jahphut's editorial team and CreateSpace editors.
Cover design by Dzine by Kellie—www.dzinebk.com.
Cover Model-Sumore. Photographed by Tatianna Lavin of TL Glam Studio.
Printed in the United States of America.

All rights reserved. No part of this publication can be reproduced, stored in a retrieval system, or transmitted in any form or by any means—for example, electronic, photocopy, or recording—without prior written permission of the publisher.

This book is dedicated in loving memory of my dear
friend Shelly.

…And to all the cancer warriors and survivors.
Keep fighting, stay strong, and never give in.

ACKNOWLEDGEMENTS

I wish to thank my Mommy and my Best Friend for always keeping me encouraged, inspired and confident in my gift. Without your continuous support, the road to success would be difficult to travel.

PROLOGUE

SUMMER 2012

DA BACK WOODS

The rising humidity and high temperatures force sweltering smog into the atmosphere as the muffler on the black cargo van ricochets sparks of smoke and cancer-like fumes through the midnight-themed back roads off St. Ann's Parish. The driver inhales a long drag of ganja as the passenger sings reggae tunes in between sipping tastes of Appleton Rum from his flask.

The van driver says hoarsely,

"Mi hope dis dun take long."

The van passenger looks at the driver, singing loudly and banging his hands on the van console, nods his head, and reaches out for the joint. He takes a long drag, inhales, and then exhales while choking. He turns toward the back of the van, peers through the caged screen, and rubs his crotch while smiling.

"Weh ih deh?"

The driver turns onto a dark dirt road that is camouflaged with white bully and pigeon plum trees. The driver immediately slams on the brakes as a dog walks slowly past the van. The driver irately curses the dog.

"Disya blouse and skirt, Mon."

The driver shuts off the ignition and looks at the passenger with a blank stare. He speaks slowly, and he reaches his hand out.

"More fiah."

He grabs the ganja, inhales deeply, and then exhales. He reveals a devilish smirk through his bloodshot red eyes and looks at the van passenger.

"Leggo."

Both men step out of the van just as a black SUV backs up to the rear of the van. The SUV driver steps out of the truck, blending into the pitch-black atmosphere.

The van driver smiles and says to the passenger,

"Mi smell a scenty woman. Mon, she put on da perfume for mi!"

Just before the van driver can speak again, a petite figure is standing behind him with loaded steel pressed into his back.

The SUV driver says angrily,

"Who is this extra person? We don't need any trouble."

The van driver turns, slowly rubbing his crotch and smiling.

"Na worry 'bout it. Dis mi bredda."

The SUV driver angrily responds,

"You know I hate when you speak that goddamn patois. Speak English and learn to follow the rules. If I say come by yourself, that's exactly what I mean. I don't need too many hands in this pot. Understood?"

The van driver brushes the SUV driver's face with the back of his hand.

"No worries, Mon…I mean, Miss Lady. You are beautiful. No need to be harsh. My bredda just keeping me company. Na worry!"

The SUV driver says calmly,

"Look, I've had a bad day and a bad flight. Open the door so I can take the package up the mountain."

The van driver unlocks the cargo van doors and opens the right door, revealing a gagged and bound human package for pickup.

The van passenger speaks curiously,

"Who dis beauty?"

The SUV driver stands between the package and the van passenger and speaks sternly.

"No details, no fail. This is not your business."

The van driver walks up to the SUV driver and whispers in her ear. Then he kisses her on her cheek.

"Mi be tinking 'bout you. I tink I love you."

The SUV driver smiles and then dissolves the joy into a frown.

"Help me get the package into the truck."

As the human package is seated in the backseat of the SUV and secured for the ride up the mountain, the van driver and passenger retreat to their van.

The passenger looks at the driver and says,

"I tink mi love one."

The driver laughs slyly and responds,

"Mi too, Mon. Now fiah more."

The driver inhales, chokes, and speeds off as the van's headlights flash across the pair of black boots stepping into the SUV, displaying the image of pink wings on the heel of the black stiletto boots. The driver smiles and looks back, turns the reggae music on blast, and says softly,

"Mi too, Mon."

Chapter 1

2011

ROCKIN' HALLOWEEN MISCHIEF

The overflowing atmosphere of decorative ghosts, skeletons, gremlins, and pumpkins paint the streets and houses in downtown DC, as the city festively prepares for numerous parties at the strike of sunset. Dylan Jones, a sassy twenty-year-old, self-proclaimed diva, pulls into the underground parking garage of the Jones Obstetrics and Gynecology practice in Georgetown. She pulls her 2007 silver Lexus into a parking space close to the elevator so her five-inch-platform pointed-toe boots won't cause discomfort to her manicured toes.

She sprints hastily onto the elevator as it closes, and she notices a nicely dressed woman standing in the corner of the elevator. Dylan presses the button for the sixth floor while glancing at the gray leather knee boots worn by the woman sharing the elevator space. The skinny, black four-inch heel elongates the woman's bowed legs. Dylan's mouth salivates at the color and texture of the boot. She smiles at the woman, who is unaware of Dylan's admiration, because she's focused on scrolling through two cell phones while typing and reading information on both screens. The elevator stops on the sixth floor and both women exit the elevator and walk to the same office suite. Dylan walks in and greets the receptionist and others nearby.

"Hey, ladies...how ya'll doing?"

The receptionist and other staff return a warm greeting to Dylan. The elevator mate excuses herself as she stands next to Dylan and reaches for the sign-in sheet. The receptionist greets the woman.

"Welcome. Please complete these forms and bring them back with your ID and your insurance card."

Dylan continues to chat with the staff.

"I can't believe today's her last day in the office. What are ya'll gonna do while she's gone?"

As Dylan chats with the staff, the woman from the elevator is called back to the counter. Dylan sits down in the waiting area to avoid disrupting the office with her friendly chatter. The woman from the elevator sits next to Dylan. Dylan smiles at her and tries to engage her in conversation.

"I love your boots."

The woman looks up from her phones. She smiles at Dylan.

"Oh, thank you, sweetie. These old things can't touch the hardware you're sporting."

Dylan blushes as she takes a glance at her feet. Her pride bleeds through the compliment.

"I love shoes...since I was five I've had a weakness for sexy shoes. My mother swears I'm an addict."

Dylan chuckles as she starts to warm up to the friendly woman.

The woman becomes intrigued. She responds,

"Addiction? Really. Well I think you're in the wrong doctor's office."

Dylan laughs.

"No, I'm here to pick up my mom…but I'm curious, why are you here? They only treat elderly…well not elderly, but senior-aged women."

The woman grins.

I'm Dr. Lynette Roberts. And you are?"

Dylan responds,

"Hi, Dr. Roberts. I'm Dylan Jones. This is my mother's practice."

Dr. Roberts smiles with intrigue and curiosity,

"Oh wow, you're Dr. Jones's daughter. Beautiful."

Just as the two women start to deepen their exchange of thoughts, a nurse calls Dr. Roberts to follow her behind the mahogany shellacked doors.

Dylan waves to Dr. Roberts as she strolls behind the closed doors with the nurse.

"Tell my mom I'm out here waiting patiently."

Dylan looks at the receptionist, looks at her watch, and laughs to show she's annoyed.

"Why does she have me rush here and she's still working?"

The receptionist smiles and chuckles.

"Dylan, even I know to tack on an hour to your arrival time."

Dylan starts chuckling as she grabs a few magazines to read. Dylan's boredom is interrupted by her singing iPhone.

"I just called to say hello…"

Dylan glances at the caller ID on the screen. The words, *Fatty Girl* flash across the screen. Her face fills with excitement.

"What up, Fatty…what's shaking?"

The voice of the caller on the other end of the phone can be heard throughout the waiting room. The shrieking and laughter have Dylan returning giggles and high-pitched chatter.

3

"Yes, girl...I can't wait for tonight. Gotta find something to wear...OK, let's go up there. I'm at Mommy's practice. Come up here."

Dylan ends the call. She smiles and stares back at the elderly patients, who are staring back at her with contentment. Dylan rummages through her purse and finds a pack of chewing gum. She pops two sticks in her mouth to prevent her sharp tongue from spewing disrespectful words at the waiting elders.

As Dylan patiently waits for her mother to appear in the waiting area, Dr. Carmen Jones, a wild and frisky sixty-year-old, sits at her desk in the back office surrounded by four walls filled with awards, certifications, diplomas, and family photos. She is staring at her computer screen, sipping on her coffee, delicately rolling her fingers through a small section of her brown curly hair, as she struggles to compose an e-mail. She periodically untwists the cap off a bottle of Jamaican rum cream and pours a small dollop into her coffee, in between reading the e-mails in her in-box. She mumbles as she reads.

"It's been a long time. I tried to stay away. I'm back, and there's nothing that will send me running."
Just as she attempts to compose a reply, three knocks echo outside her office door. She quickly clicks on the screen displaying her favorite Texas Hold'em game. The nurse interrupts.

"Dr. Jones, your three o'clock is ready in examining room number three, and your daughter is in the waiting area."

Carmen waves the nurse off, leaving her hand midair, signaling she'll be ready in five minutes. She stares intensely at the screen and opens the e-mail again. She stares at her husband's picture facing her on her desk, exits out of the e-mail, takes one last swig of her rum-flavored coffee, and pops a peppermint into her mouth. Five minutes later she walks into examining room number three and greets her new patient.

Thirty minutes later, Dylan is still sitting impatiently in the waiting room, popping her chewing gum. Just as she contemplates leaving to find something else to get into, a sassy young woman rushes through the doors of the doctor's office.

"Psst...'Ey, D. Wake up. You ready?"

Dylan lifts her head up and sees her best friend, Jazmine, standing tall in her camouflage cargo pants, olive militant boots with four-inch platform heels, and a black leather jacket.

"OMG...did you create new stops on the subway? You were just two stops away. You should've just driven...what took you so long?"

Jazmine plops down beside Dylan.

"Girl, I met this dude who gave me a ride up here. He is so cute."

Dylan shakes her head.

"I should've known something was up."

Jazmine opens her purse and pops a piece of chewing gum in her mouth. She winks at Dylan and says proudly,

"I learned from the best...get in and get all I can get to benefit my current situation. Why use up my whole smart trip card or my gas if a gentleman offers me a ride in his shiny carriage?"

Dylan smiles.

"You make me proud."

Jazmine looks around the office and notices the three elderly women sitting across from them with their noses flared upward. She slows down her chewing and begins popping loudly. She grins and stares back at Dylan.

"How long you gotta sit here waiting on Mama Carmen? What she need you to do?"

Dylan stretches and yawns.

"Yo, I don't know, but she is short. I've been sitting here I know an hour. Let's roll. I need my outfit for tonight. By the time we get back, she'll be ready."

Dylan stands up, stretches some more, and heads out the door with Jazmine. She stops abruptly, backs up, and yells toward the receptionist.

"Tell my momma her chariot waited and will return."

Two hours later, Dylan and Jazmine are walking through the mall in Bethesda, Maryland, carrying bags of shoes and clothes for their evening activities. Dylan's phone rings, and she notices she's missed three calls. Her mother's picture flashes through each ring. She stops her shopping stride and answers,

"Hey, Mommy, you ready?"

Carmen is screaming and cursing multiple levels of disappointment through the phone. Jazmine sits down beside Dylan and laughs through every expression Dylan displays as she digs deep for remorse after leaving the office without her mother. As soon as Carmen hangs up on Dylan, the two girls head back to Dylan's car to return to the doctor's office.

As Carmen continues to wait for her unreliable ride, she closes out all of her cases for that day. Then she cleans off her desk in preparation for her sabbatical. The office manager and the receptionist help Carmen lock up files she doesn't need, and they chat with her as she waits for Dylan. As Carmen chats with her team, she notices her in-box is filled with five more e-mails from an admirer. She decides to reply to the one she received earlier that afternoon. She pulls out her glasses from her purse and begins typing.

Just stop. You're too old...we're too old to act like school-aged kids. Just stop. He'll kill both of us.

Just as she finishes typing, Dylan and Jazmine burst through the office door, pleading for forgiveness.

Carmen looks at them suspiciously and rolls her eyes. She attempts to click *send.* She stands up and gives the girls instructions to grab a couple of boxes and to wait for her in the waiting area. Carmen disappears into her private bathroom. When she returns, Dylan is sitting at her desk, spinning around like a child on a merry-go-round.

"Dylan, you don't listen. Why are you in my chair? Grab the damn boxes, and let's go."

Carmen rushes over to the computer to close it out and notices she didn't click the *send* button, and panics. She attacks Dylan, accusingly saying,

"My files and e-mails are confidential. Why would you snoop?"

Dylan, annoyed and confused, just laughs.

"Ma, I know you're mad about earlier, but you are tripping. Why would I want to snoop on your patients?"

Relieved that her e-mail wasn't discovered, she clicks *send,* and closes her computer down. She stacks an extra box on top of the one Jazmine is already carrying, and the trio exits the office.

Jazmine looks at Dylan, laughs, and says,

"I guess she really needs this sabbatical. Staring up old coochies all day must be taking a toll on her."

Carmen hears the pair of misfits laughing, turns to both of them, and snares,

"Go to hell, you two...one day you'll have old coochies too."

Four hours later Dylan is pulling out of her driveway, headed back to DC, to meet Jazmine. She steps onto the lot of Club Nine and drives toward the back where the bass and percussion of radios ricochet off the walls of the aluminum gates surrounding the club. Dylan seeks out a parking space close enough to ease out of at the end of the night. She recognizes her best friend, Jazmine's, 2008 gold Honda Accord and slides her silver Lexus in between Jazmine's car and a blue Escalade.

As soon as she shifts the gear into park, she rummages through her purse to look for her makeup bag to touch up any imperfections. She checks her coal-black curly hair and shakes more volume into her thick layers. She pulls out her favorite hot pink lipstick, paints on a delicate layer, and softly mashes her lips together. Satisfied with her look, she tops it off with a psychedelic dot of pink lip gloss to give a fluorescent glow to her perfectly sculpted heart-shaped lips.

Dylan beeps the horn to gain Jazmine's attention. She suspects her best friend is indulging in her daily ritual before a set onstage, since the tinted windows are rolled up and the car is running. Jazmine rolls the window down and a cloud of smoke drifts from inside, floating toward Dylan's car.

Jazmine's spunky personality halts for a second, as she coughs through the smoke.

"What's up, mamacita? Took you long enough."

She puffs two times quickly. Dylan laughs.

"Damn, bitch…you couldn't wait for me?"

Dylan steps out of her car, straightens her short jean mini skirt, and pulls her white-and-black striped tank top down under her black denim-studded vest. Her tank top stops slightly above her tightly toned abs. She looks at her feet to make sure her studded leather boots are intact, and she grabs her purse from the backseat. She notices the driver in the blue Escalade parked beside her is staring at her. She winks at him and turns to open the passenger door to Jazmine's car. Jazmine screeches as Dylan sits inside.

"Hot mamma on the set. Look at you, looking all sassy with the miniskirt on."

Dylan pries the joint out of Jazmine's right thumb and index finger and pulls in a long drag. She notices Jazmine has on her black knit gothic fingerless glove. She stares at the puffy flesh peeking through. She hesitates and then brushes off the dark thoughts. She smirks at Jazmine and says,

"Damn, this is good. Who hooked you up?"

Jazmine laughs slyly while pulling the material up past her wrist. She says,

"As if I would tell the chief of police's daughter who my hookup is."

Dylan defensively stares at Jazmine.

"Oh, go to hell."

Jazmine apologetically looks at Dylan.

"Sike, don't be so sensitive. It's the dude Dino. Seriously, I just like fucking with you. You get so mad and so serious. I know you're not a good girl…but I think you wanna be."

Dylan rolls her eyes at Jazmine.

"I don't think being good is in my blood. But I wouldn't mind trying it out sometime."

They both laugh out loud. Dylan pauses.

"Wait, who is Dino? Have I ever met him?"

Jazmine responds,

"Yes, every week. You know—the bouncer. He gets weak around me every time I stand near me. So it was easy for me to use what I got to get what I want."

Dylan smiles proudly.

"Sweet. I've taught you well. Keep up the good work, kid. Now let's get inside to warm up for our set."

The girls step outside the Honda Accord, giggling. Jazmine notices the Escalade driver staring in their direction.

"I see you got an admirer."

Dylan pops the trunk to her Lexus and grabs her guitar bag. She looks around the parking lot, searching for the special pair of eyes.

"Who?"

Jazmine walks closer to her and turns her body back in the direction of the Escalade.

"Over there in the Escalade."

Dylan looks unimpressed.

"Oh. I've seen him several times out here. I just winked at him earlier. He's cute but he don't seem aggressive enough... so he wouldn't be able to handle me. Besides, that's probably his uncle's or big brotha's truck."

The girls giggle loudly as they walk away from the parked cars. They maneuver through the groups of zombies, witches, Michael Jackson wannabes, crocheted penises, and Malibu Ken and Barbies.

The smoke-infested club is wall-to-wall Halloween freak addicts. The bar is filled with drunken testosterone-filled minds, while the estrogen-pumped pussycats and bunnies lined up, praying for a free cocktail and or a lay. The ambiance is the perfect set for the Flaming Rejects to be introduced onstage to rock the night away. Dole, the club owner walks onstage in his grunge wear, with black outlined eyes and spiked hair sprayed with green, yellow, and purple hair spray. He clears his throat quickly and speaks into the microphone, holding his beer,

"Coooominng to the stage, one of our weekly regulars. A group of sexy girls looking to cause mischief in the world. Introducing......the Flaming Rejects."

Dylan, Jazmine, and their crew of four other horny, high and socially confused girls in their early twenties run onstage and take position. Dylan stands in the center behind her drums, the microphone adjusted to her puckered pink lips. She holds her drumsticks in her hands and clicks them together,

"One, two, three…Let's go."

The percussion of the drums, congas, and guitars sets the crowd on fire. Everyone is dancing and jumping in the air to the tunes. Dylan mesmerizes the crowd with her raspy voice and her seductive lyrics.

I don't care, just want your love, I don't care, just lick me there, not just a one-time fuck, I just want your love, I don't care, I don't care, I don't care, who you pretend to be, just love me, and be tru…ly mine, I don't care, I don't care, just love me.

Dylan recognizes Mr. Escalade in the front of the crowd walking closer to the stage. He stands in a trance as she walks in front of the drums and grabs her guitar. She sings heavily in the mic, breathing and fondling herself. Jazmine walks up from behind the keyboard, joins Dylan in front, and backs her up, singing in her soprano voice. Her long orange and pink curly fro-hawk bounces uncontrollably as her short physique forces out the strongest octaves. She embraces the stolen solo and winks at Dylan. The duo's voices spark an evolution of hallucinating and gyrating in the crowd.

When the band finishes the set, Dole returns to the stage.

"Give me a loud applause for the Flaming Rejects. I think that song is going be the reason a lot of baby-making will take place tonight. Whew! I'm horny. Is everyone else horny out there?"

The crowd goes wild.

Hours later, Dylan and the rest of her band members are drinking, dancing, and throwing back shots all night. Jazmine makes her way to the back of the club with the bouncer, Dino. He's kissing all over her, and Jazmine gives in to Dino's advances.

Dylan notices Jazmine is missing and walks around to find her. She bumps into Mr. Escalade, but she walks past him. She walks into a room in the back of the club and catches a glimpse of Jazmine bouncing up and down on Dino. She giggles and then wishes she were doing the exact same thing. Just as she walks away to head to the front, she spots Mr. Escalade and grabs him onto the dance floor. She dances erotically on him, bending over, gyrating, and rubbing all over him. He smiles. She continues…and then whispers into his ear,

"What took you so long?"

He smiles. She continues to whisper in his ear.

"I like aggression. Do you have any?"

He smiles and grabs her. He walks her to the back in a corner. He kisses her, then all over her neck, breasts, and then her lips again. She stops him and says in her raspy seductive voice,

"OK, you got a little aggression. I like."

She walks away and joins the rest of her band back by the bar. The other drummer, Sandy, whispers in her ear,

"Halloween sure brings mischief out of folks."

Dylan smirks.

"Certainly does…I wish it would've brought something else out of his pants."

They both laugh and continue doing shots.

Jazmine returns from the back of the club with Dino. She displays a delightfully satisfied grin on her face.

"Ladies, check out my winnings. She displays a valve of the white devil and a bag of weed. The girls follow her to the bathroom. Dylan sits on the sofa in the lounge of the bathroom and reminisces on the quick love affair she had in the corner.

"I gotta find out his name, and then I gotta get in those pants."

Jazmine laughs as she snorts a line, and says,

"You should've just took it like I did…don't be scared."

Dylan leans in after the other four girls and completes her line, and then they all take turns pulling a drag from the weed. Everyone is floating comfortably, seeking more seductive adventure.

As the hours drag on, Dylan is spotted by the girls on the second level of the club sliding up and down a stripper pole, and singing into the ears of Mr. Escalade. A few minutes before last call, her aggressive date whispers in her ear,

"My name is Ray. Call me so we can get to know each other… really know each other."

He kisses her once more and slides his hands up her skirt, sneaks his fingers inside her thong, and slides his number between the string and her ass.

Dylan smiles and then jumps off him as if she is startled. She straightens her clothes and pulls his number out of her thong.

"Thanks. But I gotta go."

Dylan rushes outside the club, and Ray follows behind her.

"I gotta wait for my friend Jazmine."

Ray nervously says,

"I'm glad I came tonight, and I'm glad I bumped into you. I really want to get to know you, Dylan. I've admired your music for a while, and tonight you got your hooks in me with your lyrics."

Dylan, seemingly embarrassed, says,

"You're just saying that. You just want to get your hooks in me."

She laughs as she stumbles to stand upright as she continues,

"Halloween brings out the bad in people…it looks like I've been too naughty for you tonight."

Ray smiles as he helps Dylan sit in her car.

"Not at all. If you were naughty, then I was a menace."

He licks his lips, trying to appear sexy. Dylan loses interest quickly as her cell phone rings. She answers and looks away from Ray.

"Hello...Yeah, where are you? I'm in the parking lot... are you sure? All right. Call me in the morning."

Dylan looks over at Ray, and he's still smiling at her.

"Well, my girlfriend is going home with her new boo. So I'm gonna go now."

Ray pauses and then asks,

"Are you sure you can drive?"

Dylan smiles and speeds off.

Ten minutes later, Dylan speeds down a two-lane road, dodging in and out of traffic. Suddenly, the glare of multiple flashing lights in her rearview mirror blinds her.

"Fuck. Not tonight."

Dylan increases her speed and spins out of control, landing in a ditch off the side of the road. She immediately shuts off her lights, hoping the cops don't discover her spinout. Five minutes later, Dylan's car is surrounded by Metropolitan Police. They pull her out of the car and lay her facedown on the unusually warm pavement.

The next morning, Dylan awakens in a VIP cell, with pillows and plush blankets. All of the police officers are being extra nice to her. As soon as the treatment seems too good to be true, it dissolved quickly as she picks up the screaming tone of her father, Chief Jonathan Jones.

His sixty-year-old deep voice mellows when he sees her sitting Indian-style on the hard aluminum bed.

"Dylan, before you utter any lies, listen to what I have to say. You are no longer a baby, a child, or even a teenager. Your clock is ticking. Get your life together. I will not be on this earth one day to save you from your decaying habits. I hear you were high last night, driving recklessly. Enough is enough. Shape up or you will be shipped out."

He kneels down in front of her, and kisses her forehead. Dylan's eyes fill with tears.

"Daddy, I'm sorry. I am going to change my ways. I don't want to keep disappointing you."

Jonathan softens with her tears.

"Baby, the disappointment should be the least of your worries. You can't keep up with this behavior. The partying hard, drugs, and alcohol will one day land you in the wrong district or another city where my name doesn't mean a can of beans...and you will be treated like a common criminal... I need you to create a plan. You gotta do something productive other than playing in the band. You gotta do something meaningful. Use your writing to get your own money."

Dylan bats her one remaining false eyelash for sympathy. Chief Jones continues,

"I need you to pick one. College, the academy, something. You'll be twenty-one in a few months. The clock is ticking. Choose now or I will choose for you, as I should've done when you finished high school. I let your mother convince me that you needed a break. Look what this break has cost you."

Dylan cries hard, and Jonathan consoles her.

"Clean yourself up, and I'll have one of the rookies take you home."

Dylan follows her father out of the cell and waits in the lobby for one of his chosen rookies to escort her home.

Dylan turns to her father and winks her eye at him apologetically.

"I love you, Daddy. I promise I'll change."

Jonathan sighs as she exits the station, and he whispers to himself,

"I sure hope so...I sure hope so."

Chapter 2

I WILL...FOR SHOES

The scorching sun, clear blue skies, and open road present the perfect day of leisure for Washingtonians, looking for an excuse to enjoy a beautiful Saturday afternoon—just three weeks before Christmas, and record-breaking mild seventy-degree temperatures. The sun gleams over the gated community of Waldorf, Maryland, with remnants of high mortgages, depleted property values, and empty foreclosed homes. Many families who once lived prosperously, walked away from a soul-shaking choice of survival versus *keeping up with the Joneses*. Fortunately, those who survived, sit on their porches enjoying the mild weather and craving more days of triumph and victory...the Jones family in particular.

A bare-naked Dylan stands in her bathroom looking into the full-length mirror. Dylan gives herself a glance over as she grooms herself with sweet vanilla-scented lotion for her cupcake-sized breasts, plump shaped butt, and muscular toned extremities. She rubs shea butter for the entrance to her jewel box, and Issey Miyake perfume behind the nape of her neck and center of her navel. She tops the hygienic process with a few strokes of cherry blossom lip gloss across her heart-shaped lips, and then she blows a kiss at her reflection as she struts to her closet to retrieve a white T-shirt with a heart covered in silver glitter. Dylan looks at her stainless steel Gucci watch to estimate how much time she has left before her on-again-off-again twenty-year-old boyfriend, Ray Kendrick, would arrive to celebrate their two-month anniversary. She had just enough time to search for her favorite dark-blue pair of skinny jeans that would accentuate her thighs and hips. Twenty minutes later, Dylan finds herself in the center of a pile of clothes that have tumbled out of her closet, realizing that her jeans are being tossed around in the dryer in her basement.

Dylan quietly rushes downstairs to the laundry room, attempting to avoid her mother, Carmen Jones, who is in the living room, sitting in a cloud of thick cigarette smoke that encircles her dark-brown long curly hair. Carmen sits hunched over in an oversized T-shirt and baggy sweatpants that hide her hips, wide from baring children, in front of the computer playing Texas Hold'em.

Carmen loudly says,

"What type of trouble are you about to dig into?"

Dylan responds,

"Trouble? Those days are over. I'm a grown woman…a reformed yet sexy woman. No more trouble for me."

Carmen slyly says,

"If you're so grown, why aren't you in your own crib? I got rid of one crumb-snatcher; now it's time to flip the nest so me and your daddy can retire."

Dylan responds,

"Ma, your wig is lopsided."

Dylan walks over to her mother and straightens her wig.

"Thanks. Your daddy shook things up this morning, and my wig got caught in the crossfire—whew! That man can still get down and dirty at sixty like he could when we were your age."

Dylan continues talking.

"Retire—don't you have to work to retire? You've been on sabbatical for two months and now you're talking retirement."

Carmen laughs and continues to cough through her laughter.

Dylan mumbles under her breath,

"Old naked asses. That should be illegal."

Carmen continues speaking,

"Dylan, take your smart ass on wherever you're going. I'm at the age where I can make the choice to work or take a sabbatical. I am the boss."

Dylan answers,

"I guess if I spent over thirty years looking between puckered lips and inside a variety of lotus flowers, roses, and tulips connected to elderly coochies...I'd need a break too!"

Carmen responds,

"I need a break from you! You need to be registering for school, or the academy. Your daddy would love that. Do something with yourself instead of spending our money."

Dylan responds,

"I got a plan, Ma. I just need a few more months to make an impact. I've been writing a lot, and hopefully the band will catch a few breaks."

Carmen smirks and says harshly,

"You have always been a dreamer. A bad ass—but a dreamer. You need to be a productive citizen and bring a paycheck inside these walls. Not daydreaming on how life will be as a rock star. Your time is limited in here, chick. Daddy is gonna smack the whip down on you real soon. That twenty-first is right around the corner. Take heed."

Before Dylan has a chance to respond, the virtual player on the computer makes a move that steals Carmen's attention away from Dylan, so Dylan proceeds to the basement with a frown on her face and malice in her heart.

Dylan mumbles,

"I gotta get out of this house before I end up like her crazy ass—I hope it ain't contagious or hereditary."

The cobalt blue Electrolux front-load dryer slows in rotation as Dylan steps off the last squeaky step in the basement, in pursuit of her prey. Dylan pulls the warm jeans over her calves and thighs without interruption until they reach her hips. She preps her ankles for the sumo wrestling stance, stomps her right foot, followed by her left, then leans forward slightly with gravity between her arch and heels. Dylan smiles slyly as she visualizes a perfect ten hovering above her head as she glances at her Coca-Cola-bottle-shaped torso in the glass door of the dryer.

She glances at her watch as she sashays up the basement steps en route to her bedroom to complete her runway look. She walks directly to her walk-in closet to grab a pair of her prized possessions...her stiletto shoes and boot collection. Dylan stares at the wall-to-wall stacks of clear shoe containers and designer shoe boxes. Suddenly she spots two shipping boxes with three bold letters labeled on both sides of the boxes stuffed in the back of the closet.

Dylan whispers loudly,

"FSW...what is this? I don't remember ordering anything."

She aggressively grabs the box from the corner and rips open the box from the sides. Two shoeboxes tumble out, revealing two pairs of platform stiletto surprises. One black and gray monochromatic bottom, magenta suede peep-toe ankle boot with a gold horizontal zipper across the center, and one black denim ankle boot with a folded collar with an interior pink and black comic strip pattern. Dylan's lustful eyes brighten up as she scratches her head and says excitedly to herself,

"Well, hello..."

Dylan slides her anxious toes inside the magenta platform peep-toe ankle boots, and she becomes inebriated off the new shoe fumes. Dylan's hips begin to gyrate as she glances at herself in her full-length mirror. She continues to engage in a solo conversation.

"Damn, you look good, girl. I can't wait to pound the sidewalks with you."

Dylan gives herself one last stamp of approval while staring at her reflection. Her cell phone rings. Excitedly, Dylan answers,

"Helloooo..."

Suddenly her smile turns into a twisted curl of disappointment as she discovers the caller is her best friend, Jazmine. The sound of Jazmine smacking on chewing gum scratches Dylan's eardrum like jagged nails scraping a chalkboard. Jazmine proceeds to speak loudly through the phone,

"Hey, playa...what's up with you today?"

Dylan sucks the air through her teeth to alert Jazmine that she is annoyed. Then she sarcastically responds,

"Hey...Imma have to call you back. On my way out."

Jazmine ignores Dylan's cues.

"Wait...where are you going? We got practice tomorrow. The girls want to go over new material."

Dylan's annoyance grows rapidly and she begins pacing back and forth, while pausing briefly every ten seconds to check the landline caller ID to see if Ray has buzzed the line to gain access into the community.

Dylan pauses and responds,

"You know, my dad has forbidden me to play after the Halloween incident. I haven't been able to convince him to lighten up yet."

Jazmine says,

"New Year's Eve. It's at Club Red in NW."

Dylan says,

"Look, we'll talk about this later. Ray is picking me up, and he should be here any second.

Jazmine asks,

"Is he outside?"

Dylan responds,

"No, I said he is picking me up."

Jazmine slyly laughs and responds,

"So don't rush me off the phone! I thought ya'll were over. I guess you don't get tired of running back and forth into his conniving arms?"

Dylan zones out to the chatter spewing out of Jazmine's mouth as a flash of unfamiliar circumstances plays slowly in her mind with images of her wearing all black with hot pink stilettos accentuating her physique, while dancing onstage in a club. Jazmine's words fall quickly past Dylan's ears until she hears a loud pitch of derogatory lingo halting inside her eardrum as Jazmine's voice shatters through Dylan's skillful art of tuning out unnecessary chatter. As soon as Jazmine takes a deep breath to refuel her lungs with oxygen to increase the volume for attention, Dylan peers through the bedroom blinds and successfully catches a glimpse of a shiny navy-blue Escalade pulling into her driveway.

Dylan responds,

"Look, I gotta go. Ray is here. I can't keep him waiting, especially since my daddy will be home soon.

Jazmine, answers curiously,

"Why do you even bother trying to keep them away from each other? I know you are a daddy's girl, but damn, grow some balls and stand up for who you love."

Dylan annoyingly responds,

"I just grew a pair. Bye."

Dylan slams the phone down and anxiously grabs her purse and gray leather jacket. She dashes out the front door. She locks eyes with Ray and begins to slow down her haste to power up her dramatic walk down the walkway to the blue shiny carriage. Ray pulls his shades down below his nostrils to get a crystal-clear view of Dylan's thick thoroughbred thighs as her dark-blue skinny jeans enhance the firmness with each step. Dylan notices Ray's mouth is watering with each strut, so she pauses for a second, spins in place and continues her strut down the front porch steps toward the driveway. To increase the dramatic flair of her strut, Dylan snaps backward quickly to force her voluptuous thighs and butt to bounce...but misses her mark and tumbles over into the perfectly cultivated landscaped front yard beside Ray's driver's side door.

Ray's lustful stare immediately turns into an expression of shock and humor. Dylan lays facedown on the front lawn of her house, laughing hysterically, cuing Ray to laugh with her and not at her. Ray steps out of his truck, planting his gray canvas Fendi tennis shoes onto the running board. He jumps down and grabs Dylan's hands to help pull her off the embarrassing grass-stained runway.

Ray laughs hysterically and says,

"It's moments like this that make me want to marry you one day."

Dylan smiles and pulls Ray onto the ground with her.

"So what are you waiting for?"

Ray responds,
"Too soon and we're too young, and..."
Dylan says,
"And what?"
Just before Ray has a chance to respond, an unmarked car pulls into the driveway. Ray quickly jumps up off the grass, brushes off his light-blue antique-washed denim jeans and black leather motorcycle jacket. He rushes to the driver's side of his truck, hops onto the running board, and slams the driver's side door. He responds to Dylan,
"And he's the other reason."
Ray closes the door, leaving Dylan to gather herself from her fall. A clean-shaven, dark-haired Chief Jonathan Jones pulls into the driveway. His salt-and-pepper patches on both sides of his head, lighten from the sun as he steps out of his light-blue Grand Marquis. Chief Jones walks up to his daughter and speaks sternly while helping her up off the front lawn.
"Is there a problem here, baby?"
Dylan responds innocently,
"No, Daddy, I'm fine. We were laughing because I fell... How was your day, Daddy?"
Jonathan pulls his sunshades down to the tip of his nose and stares directly at Ray when he says in a cocky tone,
"Long, hard, and rewarding. Caught a lot of bad guys and got a few cases bubbling over to the boiling point."
Ray stares straight ahead, and he coldly asks,
"What's up, Chief Jones?"
Jonathan walks Dylan over to the passenger's side of the vehicle, kisses her forehead, and smiles slyly as he walks toward the front porch before speaking.
"Dylan, you make sure you hurry back home. I want to tell you about a nice, well-respected, well-groomed young

man that keeps asking permission to date you...he's a law-yer. He's like a son I never had. I think it's time for you to meet him."

Ray starts his engine, revs it twice, and puts the truck in reverse, gassing the truck at forty miles per hour down the driveway.

Ray's anger and frustration toward Jonathan Jones force his foot to lean into the gas pedal, violating the speed limit signs in the community. Ray slows down as he approaches the security booth. The security officer walks out and shakes Ray's hand. Ray grins, nods his head, and beeps the horn as he exits the gate.

Dylan says with clarity,

"So that's how you got through the gate. Who is he? I've never seen that guard before."

Ray ignores Dylan, and the couple rides in silence for the first twenty minutes after exiting the community. Dylan pulls her sunglasses out of her purse, pulls a stick of Doublemint chewing gum, pops it into her mouth, secures her seatbelt, glances out the window, and participates suc-cessfully in Ray's silent treatment. Ten minutes after she gets settled, Ray's cell phone rings. Dylan tries to glance at the number from her peripheral view as Ray reaches for it from the dashboard. Ray ignores the call. Five minutes later, the cell phone rings again. Dylan becomes agitated and reaches for the phone. Dylan aggressively says,

"Who the hell is that trying to reach you?"

Ray snatches the phone from her grip. He stares at her with spite and says roughly,

"How much do you love me?

Dylan rolls her eyes.

Ray smirks.

"How far would you go to make me happy?"

Dylan hesitates before speaking. She rolls her eyes to the right to think of a clever answer. She responds,

"As far as my physical ability to control the outcome. Why?"

Ray responds,

"So if I told you that the only thing that would make me happy is for you to leave town with me and start fresh in another city, would you?"

Dylan pulls her sunglasses off, bats her false eyelashes with joyous desire, and says,

"As long as my shoe supply doesn't decrease. Sure, why not."

Ray becomes agitated and starts raising his voice. Ray angrily says,

"I think the only reason your ass is with me is for the perks."

Dylan gives Ray a smirk and softly says,

"I may be young and dependent on others for the finer things that satisfy my appetite for material things. But don't forget, you aren't the only man in my life. All I have to do is ask, and the funds are limitless."

Dylan reaches forward and turns up the volume to the stereo to avoid any backlash for her response and to avoid the fifth argument and breakup of the month. She pulls her sunshades back over her eyes, and she continues to pop her chewing gum to ignore the lethal stare she senses from Ray's flaring nostrils. Dylan lays her head against the butter-soft leather headrest to enjoy what is left of the perfect sunny December afternoon drive. Ray is jamming to his favorite Go-Go CD, and the vibration of the bass and drums is forming magnetic fields around her eyelids and circling her inner eardrums like lullaby tunes forcing her into a deep slumber.

An hour later, Ray drives over uneven gravel, forcing the Escalade wheels to wobble forcefully side to side. Rob pulls in front of a building. He turns off the engine and leans over toward Dylan, rubbing her hand, and speaking softly into her ear, saying,

"Hey, sleepyhead. Wake up…you know I love you—right?"

Chapter 3

BONNIE AND CLYDE

Dylan wakes up with drool dried to her chin and a damp jacket collar from her deep snooze. Dylan looks around in confusion. She snatches off her sunshades in anger as she realizes the sun has been kissed and tucked in for the night by the moon. She notices a bunch of dilapidated buildings, broken windows, and graffiti-covered signs. Dylan stretches and speaks slowly.

"Where the hell are we? What happened to our romantic afternoon drive?"

Ray calmly speaks to Dylan,

"Look, good things are happening. I want you to be a part of it. I can take care of you. I'm making money, lots of it. I know my money don't mean a lot since your pops gives you the world—his world. That shit ain't goin' last for long, especially on a cop's salary. I want you by my side as I grow my empire. I want you to be my Bonnie, and I'll be your Clyde. We can do this."

Dylan's confusion increases. Dylan says,

"Do what? Bonnie and Clyde, empires—What the hell are you rambling about? I can't be a part of nothing illegal. My daddy would have my head on…"

Ray angrily responds,

"Your daddy—your daddy. Fuck your daddy. All that rambling he did about some law student. I'll take that dude down in the street and teach him a new version of the law."

Dylan responds,

"You are so disrespectful. Take me home...back to my daddy!"

Ray smirks, and mumbles. Then he says,

"Look, I just want a chance to prove to you I'm as good as the other dudes your daddy got lined up for you. I'm making moves. This shit right here is only the beginning. I'm moving up in rank, and I'm thinking about relocating, starting over, building a big empire. So, you're either wit' me or against me. You decide."

The couple sits in silence for a few seconds before speaking. As soon as Dylan fixes her lips to speak, Ray turns to her and says,

"Sit tight. I gotta run inside, handle a few things, and we can finish talking about our future. Be right back."

Ray jumps out of the truck, leans inside, grabs the keys, and locks Dylan inside to ensure she stays inside and doesn't leave him. Ray arms the alarm and rushes up the steps to the side door of the warehouse, toward the loading dock. Dylan notices someone peering out of the door, but she ignores the silhouette, and pops a fresh piece of chewing gum into her mouth and begins cracking and popping the gum with attitude. Dylan pulls the mirror down from the visor, grabs her makeup bag to freshen up her eyes, removing the eye boogers from the corners with her makeup remover wipes, and adds a fresh layer of mascara and eye shadow.

A cargo van pulls off the duly lit freeway onto a dirt road. A cloud of dust encircles the van as the tires slowly roll over gravel and mud. Just as Dylan rolls her favorite lip gloss across her puckered lips, she glances through the mirror and notices a white cargo van pulling into the warehouse parking area. The van stops abruptly, pulling in two spaces to the right of Ray's SUV. The driver reaches for a tightly rolled "white boy" lying on the dashboard, lights the tip, shuts his eyes, inhales, and just as the driver begins to release the smoke—two sets of headlights reflect from two black SUVs through the rearview mirror, pulling in simultaneously to the left of the cargo van. The drivers of all three vehicles step out of the vehicles. Each driver is dressed all in black, brandishing weapons attached to their hips and strapped around their shoulders.

Dylan cracks the window to hear what the men are saying. The cargo van driver walks toward the two black SUVs and begins speaking.

"Let's do this."

The two black SUV drivers shake hands. Dylan notices one of the drivers has a feminine physique. The four dark, suspicious crew huddle in a semicircle and chatter among themselves. Dylan strains as hard as possible to decipher the spoken words. She hears a male voice speaking. The male voice says jokingly,

"'Ey what happened to the letters on da side of da van?"

The female voice cosigns in response,

"Looks like 'Bull Whore House,' instead of 'Fabulous Shoe Warehouse.'"

Dylan's mind flashes the acronym FSW and remembers the brown shipping boxes she found hidden in the back of her closet that housed the shoes she is currently wearing. She whispers to herself,

"So that's what FSW stands for."

Dylan slumps farther down in the seat when she notices her cell phone sounding off with a text message alert. She reads the message softly to herself.

"Dylan, stay the fuck in the truck. Don't make any noise. I'll be out in a minute."

Dylan's eyes begin to tear from nervousness and she frantically types a response to Ray's message. Dylan writes,

"What the hell is going on? Who are these armed men?"

As Dylan waits for Ray's response, another cargo van pulls up beside the first cargo truck. Passengers exit both vans with rifles in plain view. Ray rushes out the side door onto the loading dock and greets the suspicious armed crew. The drivers of the trucks and van back the vehicles up toward the loading dock and wait for their vehicles to be loaded. Once all the boxes are loaded into both black SUVs, all the drivers hi-five each other, climb back into their vehicles, and speed off, leaving a cloud of mixed dirt and gravel in the air to be inhaled.

Ray unlocks his Escalade, and loads ten brown boxes into the back of the truck. He peers forward, looking for Dylan's eyes, and anxiously speaks, saying,

"I'll explain. Just come inside and I'll tell you everything."

Dylan looks at Ray with doubt but exits the truck without hesitation and follows him inside the door on the loading dock. Ray walks Dylan through dimly lit halls with the stench of cardboard, dust, and chemicals swirling around in the air. Dylan focuses on everything and makes mental notes of items she bumps into through the dark journey. She grabs on to Ray's arm and stumbles in her platform heels to keep up with him. Dylan nervously inquires loudly,

"What is going on? Why did those people have guns? Who was the female? She sounded familiar."

Ray answers suspiciously,

"The less you know, the easier things will be."

Dylan notices shredded papers, dirty trash cans, broken chairs, dented file cabinets, and hanging wires as she follows the unfamiliar path throughout the warehouse hallway.

Ray slows down his pace and guides Dylan inside an office toward the back of the hallway and hugs her from behind. He whispers into her ear while gyrating and grinding on her.

Dylan fights against the natural urge to submit as she nervously asks,

"Ray, be honest. What are you mixed up in? I found a box in my closet that had the same exact letters that were written on the side of the white van."

Ray answers,

"OK."

Dylan becomes frustrated and responds,

"OK...I never ordered any shoes from FSW. I never heard of FSW. Then I find two boxes in my closet."

Ray sarcastically interrupts and says,

"By the way, you look damn good in them today."

Dylan responds,

"How did you know I was wearing a pair today? OK, now you're scaring me."

Ray strokes his beard, grabs his crotch and pulls Dylan close to him. Ray speaks softly and says,

"There is no need to be scared. Big Ray is gonna take care of you."

Still confused and skeptical, Dylan says,

"So there is some sort of illegal shoe scheme and designer shoes, and wholesale prices...but why do your clients need guns to distribute shoes?"

Ray becomes frustrated and forcefully grabs Dylan by the arms. He speaks loudly, as if he wants to snap Dylan out of a trance, and he shakes her as he speaks.

"Stop worrying about matters that don't affect you. You love shoes, I love lacing you in them."

Dylan doesn't back down. She hones in on her investigative skills. She asks calmly,

"So where do you fit in? Are you some type of warehouse thief?

Ray gets angry and begins yelling loudly. He sternly responds,

"Look, goddamn it, this is a shoe warehouse. Ain't nothing illegal 'bout distributing shoes from a warehouse to clients. You ain't never questioned where your shoes came from before, so don't question now."

Dylan's eyes begin filling with tears, and hysteria quickly sets in, setting her on a hysterical meltdown. Crying, Dylan asks,

"Why are you lying to me? I've never accepted any boxes from you with FSW. All of this time, you had me believing you were spending money on me, treating me like a princess."

Ray yells in response,

"What the fuck you want from me, Dylan? I'm not your fucking knight in shining armor. That's your father's job to treat you like a princess. You don't need my money 'cause your beloved daddy gives you whatever you want. I give you exactly what you desire."

Ray grabs his crotch and continues to forcefully speak.

"I grind this wood up in ya every time your horny ass asks for it, and when your eyes sparkle at a pair of shoes you see in the window, I make sure that sparkle never loses its shine."

Ray brings Dylan closer to him and leans her up against the wall. He whispers softly in her ear,

"I love you, and I'll do anything for you. All I want is a chance to show you—have you by my side as I build my empire."

Dylan begins to speak, but Ray quiets her by placing his index finger over her lips. He stares into her eyes intensely and continues to speak softly to her.

"The type of empire I'm building isn't important right now. What's important is having you by my side. No more of dat good-girl facade and daddy's-girl mentality. I want you to be my ride or die, bitch. You either wit' me, or you against me. You choose."

Dylan remains speechless as Ray begins to undress her. Ray hugs her tightly and asks,

"What do you choose, 'cause right now, I choose to get in between those thighs."

Dylan leans into Ray, and hoarsely says,

"Ride or die, huh?"

She rubs on his crotch and whispers softly,

"I choose this. But promise me you won't leave me."

Ray says,

"I promise."

Dylan interrupts and continues speaking.

"Shhh, I'm not finished. I'm not a snitch, but you can't ever make me choose between breaking laws and abiding by my father's laws."

Ray answers,

"I promise."

Dylan responds,

"Seriously, if you don't let me finish, I'm gonna scream."

Ray kisses her cheeks and says quickly,

"OK, I'll be quiet."

Dylan continues,

"I do love shoes, clothes, and money. As long as we are together, I'm in…of course limitless income and a life without despair is mandatory."

Ray says,

"I promise. I'll give you the world."

Dylan looks deeply into Ray's eyes to see if his words are genuine or laced with deceit. Ray pulls Dylan closer to him and says,

"I promise. You don't have to worry about anything. I'm gonna marry you, cater to you, build my empire for you, and love you for eternity. As long as I'm good...you're good."

Dylan smiles and relaxes her mind, falling under Ray's spell.

Ray's lips paint Dylan's face with soft circles of wet kisses, moving toward her ears, down toward her neck, locking her into a seductive trance. He lays her down on the couch and slowly pulls off her magenta platform peep-toe ankle boots, then her jeans, her thong, and then he plants long circular kisses on her shea butter-scented lips below her bikini line. He turns Dylan over on her stomach, and he says aggressively,

"Let me see dat ass. I've been dying to see it all day."

Ray pulls off his motorcycle jacket and rolls up his black polo shirt, tucking it under his chin. He unbuckles his belt, and his jeans fall to his ankles. He leaves on his gray Fendi tennis shoes and socks. He quickly rams his hanging fruit loins into Dylan from behind.

Dylan's seductive expression quickly turns to annoyance. She says angrily,

"You are a fucking cheat. You can't shift from licking to sticking without at least a ten-minute interval."

Ray shushes her! He then grabs Dylan's hips and her head tilts downward into the pillows of the smoke-infested, tethered couch. Ray's fingers dig deep into Dylan's hips as he tries to balance himself on the tip of his tennis shoes.

Dylan ignites a fume of sarcasm and insults Ray by saying,

"You ain't no real man. A real dude would've climbed on this mountain wearing Nike or Timberland boots."

Ray pushes into Dylan's love tunnel with all his might, slipping off his tippy-toes. Just as he reaches his climax, a round of gunshots echoes outside the warehouse and in the halls outside the office.

Ray nervously stops, saying,

"Damn. Shit."

Dylan jumps off the couch, shaking in fear. She looks at Ray's panicked mannerisms. She frantically says,

"Ray, what's going on? Who is shooting?"

Ray kisses Dylan on the cheek and whispers,

"Listen. That's my crazy-ass brother. He is mentally disturbed. Go hide."

Ray kisses her on the cheek, turns to her, and says,

"Dylan, I'm so sorry. I love you."

Dylan says,

"Sorry for what?

Ray pulls up his pants and heads toward the door.

Dylan tries to follow. She questions Ray again.

"Ray, what is going on? Don't leave me here."

Ray turns to Dylan with sweat running off his brow and panic in his eyes. His words begin to stumble as he speaks,

"Dylan, stay here. I'll come back for you. I promise."

Dylan responds,

"Wait, Ray—wait."

Chapter 4

WRONGFUL ENTRY

Ray heads out of the office, and before Dylan can grab her pants and her belongings, Ray walks back into the office backward with the tip of a black barrel of a 9 mm facing his forehead. A tall, rugged-looking man, wearing black cargo pants, a black hooded jacket, and dark shades, walks in following Ray. He scans the room and spots Dylan standing in the corner, wearing only her shirt. He looks at Dylan like a wild, hungry beast. He pushes Ray down and commands him to stay put. He says with a raspy voice,

"What do we have here? Smells like I'm late for this half-assed party."

He looks at Dylan and grabs his crotch, shifts it twice, humps the air, and says roughly,

"Hope you enjoyed yourself, young lady. If not, there's a better version here."

Dylan starts crying, shaking as if her nervous system is shutting down.

The rugged man strokes his prickly shaven beard. He walks closely to Dylan and speaks loudly but calmly.

"Don't be afraid. You're a guest. Any friend of Ray's is a friend of mine. I'm Big Rob, and you are?"

Dylan whispers through her wailing, and says,

"My name is D...Dylan."

Big Rob looks over at Ray, and punches him in the stomach. Big Rob angrily says,

"You don't follow any rules. No bitches allowed, unless you are sharing. Are you sharing, Ray?"

Ray yells at Big Rob and says,

"Look, Rob, we were just leaving."

Big Rob says,

"Oh, now you want to follow the rules. Nah! Ain't nobody leaving."

Dylan looks at Ray with confusion and anger. She begins yelling,

"Who the fuck is he, Ray? I want to go home. Come on. Take me home."

Big Rob says slowly,

"Now, now, there's no need to rush home. My lil' brother here forgot to invite me to the party. Besides, I have some business to discuss with him."

Big Rob chuckles loudly and continues. He suddenly starts sneezing and coughing and scratching his ears. He says,

"You need to clean up in here—too many particles lingering for a free high."

Big Rob sounds off an allergy mating call of snorts and snot and continues talking.

"Something occurred to me today after I got a call. It seems someone has been running a few jobs on the solo dolo without my consent. So I called a certain muthafucka, but got no answer."

Ray is staring at Dylan, trying to get her attention. Big Rob bends down and punches Ray in the head and smacks him in the face to get his full attention. Big Rob continues his rants, speaking loudly.

"When I didn't get an answer, I figured I should come down and see what was going on in my place of business…to my surprise, somebody I trusted is doing business on the side…wonder who that trusted source could be?"

Ray starts mumbling and spewing off pleas and apologies.

Big Rob interrupts the crying storm. He says,

"Shut the fuck up. You were supposed to do one thing. Gather intel. Not become the head muthafucking honcho. That's my job. You ain't me."

Big Rob glances back at Dylan, walks toward her, and holds his 9 mm to her head.

Ray begins pleading,

"Come on, Rob, she's my girl, not my partner. She doesn't know anything."

Big Rob responds,

"Really, I think she knows enough."

Big Rob looks back at Ray, points his gun toward him, and fires a shot. The bullet grazes Ray, hitting his flesh, leaving a bullet hole in the sleeve of his shirt. Rob turns to Dylan, grabs her purse, turns it upside down, and empties it. He grabs her wallet from the floor, opens it, and pulls out her ID.

Big Rob reads the information aloud.

"Dylan Jones, two-three-six-three Peachtree Boulevard, Waldorf, Maryland. Hmmm! A suburban girl. I thought you were from the city. I bet Mommy and Daddy are upper-class, law-abiding citizens."

Big Rob continues,

"I won't assume though."

He grabs an electronic device from his waist side and scans her ID. He looks at Ray and looks at Dylan and begins smiling. He says,

"Lil' bro…why didn't you tell me this was part of your plan? We hit the jackpot? I sent you after the chief of police, and what did you do? You brought me back a gold mine."

Big Rob looks at Dylan lustfully. He says,

"That shit just made my dick hard. And after I soften it up, I think I know exactly what I'm going to do with you."

Dylan starts crying hysterically, and screaming rants at Ray. She yells,

"I hate you, Ray, I will never forgive you. I trusted you, and you were trying to set up my father—for what though, for what? You'll pay."

Big Rob interrupts and speaks forcefully.

"No, lil' bitch, your father will pay. I was sixteen when he ruined my life. He's been due for a long time coming, and now he won't be able to hide under his badge."

Big Rob looks at Dylan's feet and continues,

"I see you have already started wearing our line of products, so it won't be that hard to break you in. I got the perfect job for you."

Dylan cries hard, screaming,

"NO, NO! I'm not working for you. My father will have your life in the palm of his hands and crush you."

Big Rob chuckles loudly and says,

"You don't have any other choice. I have your life in the palm of mine. You either follow my orders or watch as I pick apart your father's perfect little career…then his life."

Big Rob continues as he scrapes his index finger across his neck as if he's chopping it off. He says sternly,

"Then I'll come back for you and your big sister."

Big Rob grabs Dylan and forces her onto the couch with the familiar position of her face digging into the couch, as he pulls her hips upward in the air. His nails leave an indentation of rugged nail prints and dirt on her skin. Dylan screams in terror. He pulls her back to release her face from the folds of the couch cushion, and Dylan grabs hold of the top of the couch.

Dylan closes her eyes tightly, and as she opens her lids, she catches a glimpse of his shoes. She notices Big Rob is wearing fresh butter *Timberlands*. Dylan's expression of terror releases into a relaxed, blank stare and her lip curls upward. Her hazel-brown eyes darken, leaving no trace of a white pupil. She begins to purr like a lion in heat. Then she leans into Big Rob's strokes as he plants his feet flat on the ground to maintain the strong stance. Dylan notices his strokes are more intense than Ray's strokes. Her purrs become more tongue twisted, alerting open ears to her enjoyment. Dylan grabs hold of his hands from the center of her back and plants them on the side of her hips to gain control of her knees digging more into the couch. Suddenly, Big Rob is intrigued, and his ravenous appetite for his prey calms. He begins to slow his pace and his strokes are more subtle and circular.

Ray lies on the floor whimpering like a bullied teen. He glances at Dylan's eyes and for a split second, she appears to be different, more sensual and confident. He figures she has zoned out for survival. He begins to whimper more as he realizes her heart would no longer belong to him.

An hour later, Dylan awakes in a fetal position. She tries to move but notices her arms are tied behind her. She overhears male voices. She scans the room and notices Ray isn't on the floor whimpering anymore. Dylan hears a familiar voice. It's Ray's voice. Ray says angrily,

"I love that girl. How could you? I want to marry her."

Dylan hears Big Rob's rugged voice.

"Fuck her. Oh, I forgot, you got to it before I did."

Big Rob bandages Ray's arm like a concerned parent consoling his beaten child.

Big Rob continues,

"You gotta remember the task at hand. You can't fall in love. Get in and get out; don't collect a nice piece of trim along the way. But, bro, I gotta hand it to you...you've hit the jackpot. Scoring the chief of police's daughter—now that's masterful. Fifteen years of my life were stolen, ripped away...and I lost the girl of my dreams. All we gotta do is continue planting evidence, and bam, he's ours. Payback is a mutha..."

Ray says,

"You still haven't told me what he did, what woman he stole. Maybe I'll find her and fuck her like you just did the love of my life."

Big Rob chuckles and says,

"You can't put it on no one like I can. That bitch was enjoying this dick. I went all up in there."

Big Rob continues,

"You owe me. Going against the plan, stepping outside the rules. Packaging up product and distributing it without proper payment. You don't even know dem dudes. They could be hot-ass undercover NARCS. You out here showboating for dat bitch. Shit, how I know she ain't undercover?"

Ray yells back in response,

"She ain't hot and she ain't no snitch. She's different. Even under a cop's roof, she's still loyal."

Big Rob responds,

"Look now. You've made your point though."

Ray yells in response,

"She'll never forgive me for this. All I wanted was to be like you, big bro. You know, start my own empire like you. You could've roughed me up and took the money...but not my bitch."

Big Rob chuckles.

"Damn, you're right. Maybe next time."

Dylan is crying hysterically, trying to free herself from the bind they've tied her in. She falls over into the rusty computer table, sending a glass tumbling off the side of the table. The two conniving brothers hear the noise and rush down the hall back to the office. Dylan manages to free her hands by rubbing the tape in circular motion against a jagged piece of glass. She frantically runs down the hall toward a side door that appears to be propped open. In a split second, Dylan's escape ends when Big Rob jumps from an overlook above the door and head-butts her to end her escape. Dylan stands in shock briefly, wiping the thick blood running down the center of her forehead. Her knees buckle like a newborn pony, and her five-foot three-inch fleshy cavity falls backward like a life-size cardboard poster giving in to tornado winds.

Chapter 5

UNEXPECTED REUNION

Dylan's eyes pop open to the sounds of bluegrass music playing from an antique radio. She begins scanning the room, realizing she's facedown on a cold cement floor enclosed with iron bars. She strokes her black asymmetric bob, clearing the jagged edges from her wide eyes. Her long torso unfolds from the tucked fetal position.

She attempts to speak, but her throat is scratchy and sore. She clears her throat and raises her lungs to push out a breath of inquiries to the slouched guard sitting at a cedar wood desk with chipped edges. Dylan says,

"Excuse me, sir…Guard, excuse me. Where am I?"

The lopsided wobbly deputy leans back in his chair and chuckles loudly.

"Well, look what we have here. The hooker is alive, Sheriff."

Dylan screeches,

"Hooker? What are you talking about?"

Before Deputy Lopsided can respond, Dylan looks down at her attire and notices she has on only the magenta platform peep-toe ankle boots Ray brought her, a blue wrinkled cotton dress shirt and no underwear.

"Can you at least tell me how I ended up here?"

Deputy Lopsided chuckles again.

"Pulled you out of a black SUV alongside Route 301. You reeked of liquor and sex. Wooo! I remember those days."

He proceeds to hog spit into a cup, tilts his head back, and tosses another handful of tobacco in his mouth as a thick wad of spit hangs from his bottom lip. He wipes the slobber with the back of his hand and then onto his once white dingy-colored uniform shirt.

"Figured your long night of sexcapades left you tired and confused from that gash the size of my big toe."

Dylan's eyes start watering as she has quick flashes of a summer afternoon date gone wrong. She suddenly feels a thin stream of blood ooze down the middle of her forehead, reminding her of her run-in with Big Rob's tapered forehead. Dylan holds her head in her hands and closes her eyes. She tries to force memories of the past night to the forefront of her mind. She sees a flash of her driving a vehicle in panic. A flash of Big Rob chasing her down in another vehicle prompts more tears to flow. Dylan hears the devilish chuckle of Big Rob driving off and yelling out the window that she'll never be able to go home to Daddy.

Just as Dylan opens her eyes with buckets of water streaming from her lashes, she sees a tall, stocky white man with curly black hair, and tightly creased beige pants. He walks up to the jail cell, whistling the tunes of the bluegrass melody and swinging his keys in his right hand. He grips the neck of his cigarette, taking in a few puffs in between the whistling. Dylan looks upward as he approaches the door and inserts the key to unlock the cell. He leans inside and hands her an orange jumpsuit to save her from more embarrassment. The sheriff speaks with a high-pitched voice, halting to clear his throat as if he needs to pull up phlegm to gain an authoritative voice. He speaks with a less-squeaky pitch.

"What is your name, lil' lady?

Dylan reads the words above his pocket filled with pens. She says hoarsely,

"Why am I here, Sheriff Blake?

The sheriff responds,

"You can't answer a question with a question."

Dylan responds,

"I would like my phone call now."

The sheriff chuckles, and then the lopsided deputy chuckles.

Dylan scans the room for other hints to clue her in on what jail she has landed in.

She spots the deputy's jacket on the back of his chair.

She looks at the sheriff and softly asks,

"What am I doing in this West Virginia jail?"

Sheriff Blake takes a long drag of his nicotine stick and responds,

"You mean, what were you doing way down here in my town, with no license, and driving a black SUV filled with drugs?"

Dylan just stares at Sheriff Blake.

Sheriff Blake continues,

"Well, I know you speak English, so answer me."

Dylan begins to get angry and loud,

"What the hell—I was attacked and left stranded. I want a lawyer. I do get a phone call.

Sherriff Blake calmly responds,

"Now, now, sweetheart, I'm sure we can clear this up in no time. It's slow here, and paper pushing don't bring out the best in me. I don't want to process you or charge you for possession and prostitution. We've already taken care of those powder bricks for you. Now we just want to be compensated."

Deputy Lopsided walks up, rubbing on his dirty pants, searching for his nutsack,

"What Sheriff is trying to say is, we like having fun, and you seem like you love to have fun, so this small incident can disappear like the wind."

Dylan stands up with her back against the wall with a fighting stance.

"I be damned. You hillbilly muthafuckers ain't coming near me. Charge me. I ain't done nothing wrong but be in the wrong place at the wrong time. I'll take my chances. My father is the chief of police in DC and he'll rip the infested intestines out of your ass and leave you spitting your shit through your mouth."

Sherriff Blake stops abruptly and says,

"What you talking about—chief of police? Name-dropping don't work here in my town, sweetheart."

Dylan's hazel eyes begin to darken, and her temporal vein starts pulsating faster as Sheriff Blake walks inside the cell. Deputy Lopsided closes the cell behind him. Dylan takes off her pumps, rolls up her sleeves, and gets ready to pounce on the sheriff.

Deputy Lopsided goes back to his leaning chair and begins hog spitting while sifting around in his brown paper tobacco bag. His fat sausage fingers grip a thick helping of tobacco and he drops it in his mouth. He leans forward and turns up his bluegrass station on the radio to tune out what he thinks will be sounds of moaning and delight.

Just as he begins to hum to the tunes on the station, a tall rugged man wearing butter *Timberlands*, blue jeans, and a black sweat hood walks into the hick-town police station with a three-man entourage.

Deputy Lopsided pulls forward and leans out of the chair nervously. He looks back at the cell and sees Dylan fighting off the sheriff with every ounce of energy. He walks out to the front of the lobby. Surprised, Deputy Lopsided asks,

"Can I help you fellas?"

He hears muffled yelling and screaming behind the door and tries to talk over the commotion. The rugged man says sternly,

"I'm looking for my sister. She called last night and said she was lost—we've been looking for her all night."

Deputy Lopsided responds,

"Is that right, boy. So why do you think she's here?"

The tall rugged man looks at his entourage and nods. They immediately cock their guns behind them and the rugged man pushes the deputy down and ties his hands behind his head. He then kicks the door in, scans the back room, and sees the sheriff inside the cell facedown. A petite woman in a shirt stands over him, wiping blood off her face. Unaware that others are in the building, Dylan starts scanning the room for the keys to unlock the cell. She continues to kick the sheriff in the face and back. The rugged man is turned on instantly that such a small woman could take down such a large man. He is surprised at her abundance of confidence. He yells,

"Yo, sweet ass!"

Dylan looks up and is shocked and happy at the same time. Dylan responds,

"What the hell? What, why, I can't...

Big Rob stares at her for an instant, taking in all of her confidence. He likes that she doesn't seem timid like she was when he first met her. He grabs a set of keys off the wall, walks over to the cell, and opens the door. He grabs an orange jumpsuit off the back of the door and hands it to her. He then says,

"Here, cover up."

Dylan climbs into the oversized jumpsuit and steps into her pumps. She instantly rolls her eyes at him.

Big Rob continues as he hurries her along,

"Look here, sweetheart, there ain't no time for hmmm and huhhhhs and attitude. Let's go."

Dylan says abruptly,

"Stop calling me sweetheart. You don't know me."

Big Rob says,

"Shut the fuck up and come on."

Big Rob grabs Dylan, picks her up, and throws her over his shoulder. He gives his crew another nod, and they begin ransacking the hillbilly jail. Rob runs around the back of the building and spots his SUV. He throws Dylan in the back and speeds through the gate. Dylan is turned on and is staring at the back of Big Rob's head. Her eyes are still dark and mysterious. She notices the entourage running out of the jail with a duffel bag, heading to their truck. Big Rob beeps the horn and speeds off.

Dylan looks straight into the rearview mirror. Big Rob looks back at her.

She says nervously,

"This isn't over. I'll go to jail for sure."

Big Rob chuckles slyly and says,

"No worries...Big Rob takes care of everything."

Just as Rob speeds off the road onto the main road, the building behind them explodes, sending building pieces, steel, rubble, and orange jumpsuits in the air.

Big Rob looks back and smiles.

"No worries!"

Dylan smiles. Curious, she lets her guard down. She says softly,

"You came back for me. Why?

Big Rob responds,

"Something about you intrigues me. And business is business. You have a lot of work to do."

Chapter 6

THE REAL AWAKENING

Dylan sits back and begins to enjoy the bumpy ride home. She rubs the blood off her face and legs, as she flashes in and out of the past twenty-four hours. Dylan's eyes return to their hazel state, and her timid self-returns. Her eyes water and she begins to think about the previous night's events.

She asks,

"Where's Ray? I want to see Ray."

Rob responds,

"Don't worry about Ray right now. He's off this detail. You can't send a boy to do a man's job."

Dylan says sarcastically,

"A man's job. I haven't come across a real man other than my daddy."

Big Rob stares back into the rearview mirror and speaks authoritatively,

"Don't mix my heroic encounter with any superficial nonsense. You have work to do, and it will be done. When I'm done with you, you'll know a real man. Your daddy certainly isn't one. I bet you think you know everything about your daddy."

Dylan tears up. She yells in response,

"You will never measure up to the man by dad is—you don't stand a chance."

Big Rob turns the music up, puts on his shades, and speeds down the highway in silence for two hours. When he reaches the gated community where Dylan lives, he hands her an envelope.

Ray says,

"Open this when you get inside your house. Don't speak about anything that happened yesterday or today. I will know. Trust me."

Dylan stares blankly and says,

"How did you know where I live?"

Rob speaks,

"Like I said, trust me. I will know. I know everything."

Dylan responds,

"You do know that my father isn't the only one that carries a badge and a gun."

Rob says,

"You ask too many questions. I know your sister...better than you do."

Rob chuckles devilishly, leaving no time for Dylan to respond. He continues,

"In time, lil' girl, you'll find out everything you want to know about the fantastic duo."

Dylan responds curiously,

"So why me? Why not go straight to my sister?"

Big Rob stops at the back security gate and punches in the key code to gain access to the grounds.

Dylan is flabbergasted. She asks nervously,

"How the fuck do you know all of this information? Who gave you the code?"

Big Rob turns onto a street behind Dylan's house. He turns the truck's ignition off, steps out of the truck, and sits in the backseat with Dylan. He touches her hand, rubs her face, and then clutches her neck with force.

He says forcefully,

"Look, I like you. You're sassy, timid, fearless, and ruthless all in one big bowl of mystery and chaos. I like that."

He touches his crotch, tugs on it, and rubs it slowly. He continues,

"You handled this dick like a pro—something I'm not used to."

Dylan looks into his eyes with submission.

Big Rob continues,

"What I don't like is defiance and resistance. I mean business, and I will destroy any and all who cross me or jump in my way. What you need to know is your father will be brought down to his knees, and I will take back what's mine!"

Big Rob rubs his chin and scratches the side of his head, scanning the neighborhood. Dylan yanks her hand from Big Rob and reaches for the door handle. She attempts to open the door, and he pulls her back.

Dylan begins to scream and yell. Big Rob closes the door. Dylan responds to his brute approach.

"What do you want from me? I don't owe you nothing."

Rob leans in and speaks sternly but calmly.

"You're the perfect alternative. It's golden. My lil' brotha couldn't have given me a more better gift. Lil' bro worked so hard to get in good with the security guards here and delivered me all the intel I needed, with you as the extra prize. I gotta hand it to him. He thought of that piece on his own and didn't even tell me. I never thought we could get close to you. You are such a prized possession. Daddy is slippin'."

Big Rob smiles and continues,

"See, your daddy took so much from my life and my family. He's not who you think he is, and apparently you're not who he thinks you are. This is a win-win situation for me. Either you do what I tell you to do, and my new plan will remain in effect—or you defy me, and your precious daddy will go bye-bye for good. The evidence is stacked against him."

Rob pulls out a DVD, winks at Dylan, and says,

"And you...you really don't have a choice. Daddy's lil' girl will just be a ho. But if you go against the grain, Daddy's career is over and he will go away...far, far away."

Dylan remains silent, and Big Rob releases his grip around her neck and opens the door. Big Rob speeds off, and Dylan stands in shock as his SUV disappears.

The sun begins to set and Dylan opens the envelope. She sees a handwritten note that reads,

"I'm watching you. Remember, your father's life and career are in your hands. Follow my rules, no one gets hurt or destroyed."

She laughs loudly, and suddenly her eyes harden with dark vengeance. She slowly turns her head toward the sky, smiling cunningly. Her rude ego has awakened. She turns in a circular motion, laughing and screaming aloud,

"Big Rob, you fucking twit...I told you muthafucka my name is Demi. Thanks for the push though—you ain't got a clue."

She unzips the orange jumpsuit and steps out of it, leaving it on the curb, as she sashays up the block in her magenta platform peep-toe ankle boots and collared shirt. She continues ranting,

"Research is key...should've sifted deeper. I run this shit. Not Dylan. You've got it twisted, ain't no good girl here... that daddy's-girl image was tainted a long time ago. Ain't no muthafuckin' skin off my back. I'm back...Demi is awake and kicking."

Chapter 7

SIBLING RIVALRY

A midafternoon drug bust lands Sergeant Janay Jones, an undedicated, semi-loyal DC metro cop, in an interrogation room, preparing to pull the truth or a hot lead from a perpetrator. As Janay waits for the detectives assigned to the case to rehearse their good-cop-bad-cop routine behind the two-way mirror, she plants a few black eyes on the slimy perpetrator, ripping his fitted T-shirt.

Two thick streams of blood begin to journey out of the perpetrator's nose. A banging sound against the mirror alerts Janay that her behavior has gained attention. She stands up straight and rolls out the wrinkles in her fitted uniform shirt, rolling her hands downward from her voluptuous cleavage. She erases the dripping sweat from her brow with a swipe of the back of her hand, and she pats her freshly shaped-up curly 'fro, ensuring its carefully sculpted ringlets aren't out of place. An authoritative voice signals Janay a command through the hidden overhead surround sound system.

"Ease up, Sergeant Jones."

Janay looks toward the mirror and sighs loudly. She returns her attention to the perpetrator, raising her hand once more to leave a lasting impression. The voice appears again,

"Sergeant Jones...stand down."

Janay walks toward the door, looks at the perpetrator, and exits the room, leaving the door cracked open. Before she can step over the threshold, the detective duo prevents her from fleeing.

The lead male detective looks Janay up and down from her rugged black laced-up boots to her overly aggressive cleavage. He remains quiet, yet grins as he rubs his chin. The female detective clears her throat forcefully and says,

"Your behavior isn't part of our routine. You keep crossing the line, your days here at fifty-five are numbered."

Janay rolls her eyes, rubs her gun holster, and says slyly,

"You wish you had the power, don't you."

Janay chuckles devilishly. Just as she forces her way past the detective duo, another roughed-up perpetrator is led past them. Janay pushes the door wide open, leaving the perpetrator exposed for the passing thug.

The walking perpetrator yells out loud as he sees the other guy drinking a canned soda while being handed ice and tissues to blot away the blood from his nose.

"'Ey, you serious? This is how you repay me? Snitches get stitches, yo!"

Janay smiles and pushes her way past the detective duo.

"Looks like my job here is done."

Janay heads to the staff locker room to change her clothes before leaving for the day. As she enters the room, a group of laughing women in a huddle instantly soften their chuckles while throwing invisible daggers at her to force her to keep walking. One of the women, dressed in only a bra and her uniform pants, mumbles to the group in a whiny voice,

"I am the shit, 'cause my daddy runs the show."

The other women laugh loudly as Janay's face reddens with hatred and rage.

The woman continues to taunt Janay in her whiny voice,

"My daddy lets me get away with everything, even though I'm the worst cop in the world."

Janay responds angrily,

"Grow up, bitches, this ain't high school. I run my own show. Keep it up, and I'll be running yours too!"

Janay reaches to open her locker door, scrolling through the combination lock numbers. She opens the door forcefully and notices the ragged Scotch tape pieces securing the home-made calendar on the inside of the door. Her eyes zoom in toward the date circled in red. It reads in bold:

"December 15th—My 34th"

She quickly slams the locker door as she whispers to herself,

"I forgot my fucking birthday is tomorrow. Another lonely year."

Mad and feverishly sweating from rage, Janay decides to leave the precinct in her uniform. As she heads to her police cruiser, she bumps into a tall slender fair-skinned man dressed in the same navy-blue attire as she's wearing. In a hasty attempt to flee the scene, Janay rudely speaks as she knocks the slender man's cell phone out of his hand.

"Urgghhhh…watch where you're walking, Sergeant Foster."

Sergeant Foster widens his hazel-grayish-brown eyes and looks Janay directly in her eyes. He smiles slyly and shifts his six-foot, 180-pound frame from one bowed leg to the other. He rubs his goatee and licks his lips simultaneously.

"Sergeant Jones, bumping into you just made my day. Give me one more for the road."

Stunned by Sergeant Foster's inappropriate reaction, Janay hastens down the hall, looking back periodically, stealing a glimpse of the handsome sergeant until nothing but a silhouette glistens in her eyes.

Janay's mercury-filled anger slowly dissipates as she replays the smile Sergeant Foster unleashed with their exchange. She sits comfortably in her cruiser, turns on the radio, and starts to drive off the parking lot. Just as she accelerates, a breaking news alert cuts into the R and B music, announcing a man-hunt for a gang-related arson and robbery at a small West Virginia sheriff's department about an hour and a half outside Washington, DC. The radio DJ explains that a petite woman in an orange jumpsuit and heels is a person of interest, along with an entourage of black, tall, strong men driving black GMC SUVs. Janay listens intensely and says to herself,

"Well other than the orange jumpsuit and heels, their description describes everyone that's driving down the street... dumb-ass civilians and their half-assed reports."

Janay continues to drive off the parking lot, and she decides to head to her parents' house to visit. Just as she pulls into the gated community and punches the security code to enter the premises, she notices a black SUV. She laughs out loud to herself.

"Hell, this could be one of the suspects."

Just as the gate lifts for Janay to enter, the black SUV pulls across from her and waits for the gate to lift to exit. Janay tries to catch a glimpse of the driver, and just as she realizes the tints on the driver's side window are too dark, the window rolls down just enough for her to see the driver's eyes. The driver of the SUV holds up two fingers toward the security guards and peels off, leaving tire marks.

Janay continues to drive in confusion, whispering to herself,

"That can't be him. It just can't be. I thought he was dead. No, I'm convinced; it's not him."

Janay pulls in front of her parents' house and notices her sister, Dylan, standing outside in a blue-collared shirt and her magenta platform peep-toe ankle boots. Dylan is laughing and talking to the sky, and proceeds to the back gate, leaving the orange jumpsuit behind. Janay continues watching her until she is out of sight. Janay exits her cruiser and walks up to the orange jumpsuit. She smiles intensely, speaking to herself,

"This has got to be the easiest lead ever to fall into my lap. Wonder what you've been up to, Ms. Dylan."

Janay enters the front door to her parents' house and over-hears the sound of two screeching hens arguing.

Janay interrupts with authority,

"Now hold the fuck up with all of this noise. What the hell is going on in here?"

Carmen looks toward Janay and argumentatively responds,

"Who the hell you talking to like that? Have you forgotten who I am?"

Dylan's shell stands still, but her aggressive side says intensely,

"Oh, look who is here. The hero. The one with vengeance a happy trigger finger. What the hell you want—you don't live here anymore."

Janay is stumped by her mother's and sister's reactions to her arrival. She turns, equally aggressive in her stance, but with one glimpse of her mother's angry face, she backs down.

"Look, I just stopped by to see you. You sounded upset last night that you hadn't heard from this ratchet-ass heathen all night."

Carmen calms down and responds with grace.

"Well, sweetheart, just say that when you enter my home. Don't try and run my set. This nest is for me and your father to run."

Dylan's skeletal shell, covered with caramel skin, stands frozen. She looks at Carmen and Janay with disgust. She responds with malice.

"First, let's get it straight...Dylan has checked out. I'm back on the set. But if you've forgotten, let me refresh and reset the rules. I'm the head bitch in charge. When you look at me, you see the timid little princess, but when I speak—remember, bitches—I'm Demi."

Janay and Carmen are standing speechless with concern.

Demi continues...

"Now you, the overaggressive cunt, don't come in here like you are the boss. There is enough trouble in here to go around."

Janay says,

"Ma, I knew something was wrong. I watched her laughing and talking to herself outside. Sneaking in the back gate half dressed. It's a good thing I'm here, 'cause this crazy bitch is a lot to handle."

Demi rolls her eyes and says rudely,

"Fuck you, Janay. You're a shit starter looking for an ass to kiss. Well, Daddy ain't here, so get the fuck out."

Carmen lights up a cigarette with her shaky hands. She says nervously,

"I wasn't ready for this today. This is really plucking my nerves.

Carmen looks at her watch again, and she continues,

"In ten minutes I gotta log on for my midday Texas Hold'em match. I know I'm going to win. So, Janay, if you aren't here for a reason, then you should be on your way. Remember, I handle Dylan, not you—that's my job, not yours."

Janay walks up to Dylan's shell, sniffs her, and begins pulling on her shirt. She sniffs her again.

"Momma, whoever this is right now...she's been a bad girl. Have you even asked her yet where she was all night? You didn't hesitate to call me when she didn't answer your calls. Now that your psychotic baby is home, nothing matters."

Carmen takes a long drag of her cigarette, looks at her watch, turns on the television, and sighs deeply.

"Go home, Janay. We are fine. I'll handle this."

Janay slyly giggles.

"I'll go, but before I do...Dylan...I mean, Demi, what is that scent you're wearing? It smells so familiar. It smells like... sex with more than one man. Were you out whoring? Is that what you, or she, has chosen to do for a living? That will really break Daddy's heart...you fucking whore."

Carmen rushes over to the two girls, raises her hand, and stands in between Dylan's shell and Janay. She begins screaming loudly, leaving a ringing in both girls' ears.

"Janay, that's enough. Get the fuck out. I can't believe you. Get out!"

Everyone becomes silent as the television flashes a still image of a female that resembles Dylan wearing an orange jumpsuit and high-heel boots. The news anchor reveals that the security surveillance is backed up from another sheriff's station in Martinsburg, and the fleet of black SUVs is being sought after in order to identify the men responsible for the senseless killings and arson.

Janay chuckles uncontrollably.

"This has got to be the best day ever. I can finally stop this lil' bitch in her path and get rid of her forever."

Dylan's eyes begin to twitch and lighten as Janay puts her in a choke hold and dangles the orange jumpsuit in front of Carmen and Dylan. Dylan screams horrifically in confusion.

"Janay, let me go. What are you doing? Let me go; you're hurting me."

Carmen screams,

"Janay, let go. That's Dylan. She's back."

Janay laughs psychotically.

"I can finally get you out of our lives. I'm taking her in."

Carmen squishes her cigarette in the ashtray and punches Janay in the face.

"I said let her go. This is your family, and you are so hell-bent on proving yourself you will risk anything to show off. You know Dylan don't have nothing to do with this."

Janay drops Dylan and curses Carmen before rushing to the door. As Janay hastily passes her mother and sister, Carmen grabs the jumpsuit out of her hand. Janay looks at Carmen with intense malice. Carmen smiles gracefully and speaks forcefully.

"If there is any involvement with Dylan, your father will handle it."

Janay's eyes fill with rage and tears. She screams at Carmen,

"I bet you didn't even remember my birthday is tomorrow."

Carmen looks toward the door with confused amazement. Janay's streams of tears and snot bombard her puckered lips.

"Of course you forgot. It's always about that red bitch over there."

She storms out of the front door.

Carmen looks down at Dylan, concerned but disappointed. Dylan lies on the floor rubbing her bruised neck. She says cautiously in a raspy voice,

"Why do you automatically look at me when trouble erupts?"

Carmen lights another cigarette, sits on the floor beside Dylan, and shakes her head.

"Shit, Dylan, what's happened now?"

Dylan stares blankly and remains silent.

"You know, we're now going to reconsider treatment. Demi came in with vengeance today, and I'm all out of options. We have your crazy, hotheaded sister running on vengeance, and flashing images of your face popping up on every news station."

Carmen reaches for her cigarette case, rummages toward the bottom, and pulls out a tightly rolled stick. Reaching for her lighter, she returns to holding Dylan tightly, consoling her with tenderness. She lights the smaller version of her cigarette. Dylan stops crying as she smells an aroma that reminds her of strong incense. She looks up at Carmen as Carmen calmly grins.

"What? Sweetheart, this is for emergencies. This old girl gotta pull out the guns and think. I'll figure it out, and Daddy will make it happen."

Chapter 8

DRUGS AND UNHAPPINESS

The morning whisper and radiance from the rising sun awakens Dylan as she lies on the floor of her walk-in closet. The aroma of roasted-bean coffee brewing wafts through the vents. Her father's voice penetrates her inner ear as she catches the gentle good-bye he sends her mother's way while exiting for his morning shift. Dylan's torso is tightly tucked under the folds of her arms and her fingers tightly clutch a red leather-bound journal. Dylan slowly rises from her tucked position and sits upright, sifting through the pages of her secretive thoughts. She notices the red and black striped ribbon is neatly tucked between two pages dating back a year and a half. Several paragraphs are highlighted in pink, enclosed with hearts, circles, and question marks. She begins to read the special entries...

August 5, 2011
I felt really weird today. I couldn't remember if I took my Aripiprazole. The bottle seems awfully full.

August 24,
Our set was strong. We played hard, and we were off da hook. We drew the biggest crowd ever. There was this sexy guy that kept staring at me all night. He didn't have the balls to speak to me. Moving on...

October 20,
I saw Mr. Sexy again after we played our last set. His eyes are
piercing, and his smile makes me moist.

October 31,
This morning was off to a weird start. Halloween is always weird,
but there is something in the air. I just got my Aripiprazole refilled,
and now I can't find it.

November 1,
I woke up in jail...again. I found hickeys on my neck, my thighs,
and breast, and Mr. Escalade's number. My father hit the fan. I
don't want to disappoint him. I have to change my bad behavior.

November 18,
Apparently I'm in love with the Sexy Man, and his name is Ray. He
buys me everything I want, including my favorite shoes. I think this
could work...for my shoe addiction anyway.

December 1,
I gave in...I gave into Ray and went against my six-month trial
period. Not sure how it happened, I just remember rocking out onstage
last night, and then waking up in a huge hotel suite. I'm suspicious as
to how he convinced me, and what the fuck I was wearing.

Dylan closes the journal and begins weeping loudly. After
fifteen minutes of snotty-nose tears, she composes herself and
stands in front of the full-length mirror to snap out of her emo-
tional slump. She leans in close and begins whispering to herself.

"What have you been up to, my dear Demi? Everyone but
me knew you had surfaced. What triggered your appearance? I
should have known something was up when I couldn't remember certain events. Especially with Ray."

Dylan begins crying again.

"Did I even meet Ray on my own? Boy did they get me. Two brothers banging me out. One better than the other."

Just as the crying gets uncontrollable, her phone signals a text message alert. It's a message from Ray.

"D…man, I'm sorry. I should've protected you. I can make it up to you. Look in your closet…I love you."

Dylan turns around to scan her closet and notices three FSW boxes with a big red ribbon connecting all three. A note is attached. She opens the note and it reads,

"D, words can't express my love for you, but I hope these can. Love, Ray."

For a quick moment, Dylan begins to slightly forgive Ray. Just as she takes a short breath to take it all in to consider, she hears a loud commotion downstairs. The sound of Janay causes the hair on the back of her neck and on her arm to stand erect. Dylan's shell stands frozen, and her eyes darken. She's armed with chaotic protection from her rival. The bedroom door is thrust open with a force that she has come to hate deeply.

Janay bursts in with her gun missing from the holster. Dylan is speechless, but Demi rises to the occasion. She says rudely,

"Bitch, weren't you banned from these premises? Your punk ass waited til Pops left."

Demi ejects a thick morning breath spit to ignite more rage from Janay, which makes her feel satisfied.

Janay's stance is steady and persistent with a focus, but spit drips down the left side of her eye. She returns her gun to the holster and pulls out her handcuffs. She speaks loudly with authority.

"Dylan and Demi, you have the right to remain silent, anything you say will be used against you in the court of law.

Demi screams,

"Are you fucking kidding me? Not my Miranda rights. Do you have a warrant?"

Carmen hears the commotion from her master bathroom as she steps out of the shower. She hastens to throw on her robe and slippers to find out what is going on. She rushes to Dylan's bedroom and witnesses Janay head-butt Dylan. Carmen hysterically yells,

"What the hell is going on here? Janay, what are you doing here? Let her go. Where is the noise coming from?

Janay harshly responds,

"I'm taking control of this situation. Exactly what should've been done yesterday. She should've been admitted to a psych ward, but unfortunately, spitting on someone, especially an officer of the law, is a felony."

Carmen is beside herself, and she can't get a grip on what's taking place. She pulls out her pack of special cigarettes to calm her nerves, but while she puffs erratically, she feels a rumble in her belly and rushes into Dylan's bathroom.

Demi laughs psychotically.

"I keep saying ya'll crooked as bitches. My name is Demi. No one in this house has good intentions except me."

Before Carmen can finish relieving herself in the bathroom, Janay forces Dylan's shell—kicking and screaming—out of the bedroom, down the stairs, out the front door, and into the back of her cruiser.

Carmen washes her hands and runs to her master bedroom to call Jonathan.

"Chief Jones, please. His wife, Dr. Jones. It's an emergency… Please have him call me ASAP."

Chief Jones enters his police station after having his monthly meeting with the mayor of Washington, DC. His mood is upbeat, and he has an itch that he's hoping Carmen will scratch when he gets home. He hopes the emergency message from Carmen on his computer screen is an invitation to role-play for an afternoon snack. As soon as he calls Carmen back, all of the police staff can hear his voice on every floor of three-story building. His office door swings open, knocking Janay's graduation picture from the police academy off his wall. His voice echoes through the hall, sending rumored messages to Janay from his office.

"Get Sergeant Jones in my office now."

Minutes later, Janay walks into his office with her hands in her pockets, her hair pulled back in a tight ponytail, and her police hat in her hand. Before Chief Jones can speak, Janay utters the most pathetic and childlike words to her father.

"Daddy, don't be mad. You don't understand. She spit on me, and she has been involved in some criminal acts."

Chief Jones stands up, and before Janay can utter another excuse, he yells at the top of his lungs the most gut-wrenching response.

"You are the worst disappointment. I don't understand you or the malice you hold in your heart for that girl. Your actions over the past few weeks around here have been stacking up, but today is the day—I've reached my limit. You are on temporary suspension until further notice. Drop your badge and your gun and get the fuck out my office."

Janay's eyes filled with rage as she yelled back at him.

"Are you fucking serious? You're suspending me on my birthday. The lil' bitch gets away with everything...including murder apparently. I'm sure you're doing nothing about her hand in all the drama that has unfolded in the past couple of days. She goes missing for days at a time, she hasn't taken her medication in many full moons, and the little bitch's demon has been unleashed, which is probably why her criminal activity heightens every day. Yet you're yelling at me. Man...you poor-ass excuse for a fucking father...don't worry about temporary. I fucking quit."

Janay storms out of her father's office and rushes to the locker room to change out of her uniform into her regular clothes. Chief Jones walks down to the lockup to get Dylan released. As soon as he walks into her cell, his eyes water as he sees his little princess balled up in a corner. Chief Jones bends down to pick her up off the floor, and he looks into her eyes while speaking softly.

"Dylan, baby, come on. Daddy's gonna take you home, but first, we're gonna go to the doctor to get you checked out. Dylan...do you hear me?"

She lifts her bloody head up and speaks.

"For the last time, my name is Demi, and I'm not an alcoholic."

Demi laughs uncontrollably and continues,

"You weren't there to protect your precious Dylan, so here I am. She's gone for now...maybe forever."

Chief Jones looks frightened for his princess. He looks into her dark eyes and pleads,

"Dylan, I know you're in there. Wake up. Wake up. As soon as we get you treated, I promise you'll get that white SUV I promised you. Just come back to me, baby."

Demi continues her psychotic laughing. Chief Jones stands up, places Dylan's body on the bed in the cell, exits, and calls for an ambulance.

Janay is peering from behind the wall, listening to her father promise Dylan the world. Her tears flow heavily. She rushes out of the police station, runs frantically down the street, later realizing she doesn't have her car, because she's been driving the police cruiser. She screams at the top of her lungs,

"Fuck you, Daddy...you never offered to buy me a brand-new car."

Minutes later, he returns and watches as Dylan's shell is laid onto a gurney and rolled out of the cell.

Janay is sitting at a bus stop nearby, guzzling a bottle of vodka and talking to herself like the winos she is used to busting for disorderly conduct. She sputters and rants continuously to herself.

"Happy birthday, bitch. That's all I wanted. I mean a cake and candles would've been good too...but no. It's always about the lil' princess. What's wrong with this picture? I'm cute. Right?"

Janay stands up and looks around like she's talking to an audience. She starts laughing uncontrollably at herself, trying to catch a glimpse of her reflection in the glass panes of the bus stop shelter.

"Hell, yeah, I'm cute. I'm fine. Gotta fat ass, but everybody rides that poor lil' miserable bitch's ass. Oh, Dylan is fragile. What about me? No one thinks about me. Well, enough of that shit. I'm reclaiming my position. Fuck you, Daddy, and your stupid-ass Texas Hold'em playing-ass wife. Bitch gonna punch me out. Fucking asshole mother. Ya'll can kiss my black ass. I'm bringing all of ya'll down. Conspiracy, access, um, I mean accessory...some shit like that."

The blazing sun begins to burn Janay's eyes as the vodka warms her extremities from the cold December weather. She sits down quickly on the bench to fight off the instant urge to puke her brains out. She catches a glimpse of the ambulance racing out of the police station parking lot headed to the hospital. Janay rushes to the curb, hurls the vodka bottle at the ambulance, and begins laughing insanely.

"The poor lil' bitch-ass princess is hurt."

She drops quickly to her knees and begins vomiting uncontrollably. As she finishes, she sits on the curb, sweating and crying. She continues to utter her chosen words of the day,

"Happy birthday to me."

Chapter 9

HIGH-HEEL THERAPY

The intermittent drip of saline filling the clear pouch catches the attention of Dylan's inner ear. Her eyes slowly open as she scans the room, noticing the dull gray walls with an embedded shadow hanging high from her bed. She widens her eyes and notices a tall, handsome man. She says hoarsely,

"Daddy, where am I? Why are my wrists tied to the bed?"

Chief Jones leans in toward Dylan and kisses her on the cheek. He speaks with empathy.

"My sweet Dylan, your alter has been a very bad, bad girl. Gotta make it right though…get you back on track."

Dylan looks down at her wrists as she tries to wiggle them loose. Her eyes fill with buckets of salt-laced tears. She closes them as they become too heavy to bear the weight of her pain and fear. She speaks slowly.

"Daddy, I promise I'll be good, just let me go home."

Chief Jones shakes his head in disagreement as a tall, slender woman in a white coat appears behind him. The middle-aged woman tugs on her stethoscope that hangs above her small preteen-sized breasts that seem to be pushed up by a black-laced push-up bra. She clears her throat in an attempt to interrupt the father-daughter reunion and says loudly,

"Good evening, I'm Dr. Lynette Roberts."

Dylan lifts her head in shock. Dr. Roberts and Dylan make eye contact. Dylan shyly says,

"I remember you."

Dr. Roberts smiles.

"Looks like my favorite shoe lover has some explaining to do."

Chief Jones steps aside to allow Dr. Roberts to access Dylan's bedside. He looks at Dr. Roberts from his peripheral vision, trying to sneak a peek at her physique. Dylan rolls her eyes in disgust for her father's rebellion against her freedom.

Dylan begins to speak as if she owes Dr. Roberts an explanation.

"I didn't get into trouble...I was attacked."

Dr. Roberts leans in and rubs Dylan's forehead.

"You'll have time to tell me all about it."

Dylan realizes she'll have to submit to her father's demand for treatment. Her eyes water as she pleads,

"Can these metal bracelets be removed? I'm not going to hurt anyone—or myself."

Chief Jones approaches the bed, detaches a wide key ring from his belt, and unlocks the cuffs.

"There you are, baby girl. Now just relax."

Dylan asks,

"So what do I have to do to be released, Dr. Roberts?"

Dr. Roberts smiles warmly at Dylan, and looks cautiously at Chief Jones. She walks toward the window and opens the curtains to bring in natural light to brighten Dylan's mood. She clears her throat as she rummages through her pockets for a pen and sits on the edge of Dylan's bed with Dylan's chart attached to a clipboard. She speaks softly.

"Ms. Jones, I'm not sure if you're aware, but I am a therapist. So...the first thing we're going to do is get you set up for a few counseling sessions. If I like what I hear, then I'll have you home by the end of the week...hopefully before."

Dylan smirks and says,

"Didn't really peg you for a shrink…especially with your shoe game. But since I value your shoe choices, I guess I can believe you'll have my head shrunk that soon."

Dr. Roberts responds,

"Yes, I'm confident I can get into your head with success."

Dylan laughs.

"I want to be home now. But you'll have me out of here in five days just as Santa squeezes down our chimney?"

Chief Jones stands up, kisses Dylan on the forehead, and excuses himself.

"Dylan, I'm going to let you two have the time you need to get you fixed. I'll be back to check on you."

Chief Jones walks out of the room, and Dr. Roberts helps Dylan out of the bed and into the wheelchair resting against the room door. She rolls Dylan down the hall onto an elevator. As the elevator rises to their destination, Dr. Roberts drives Dylan down a hall filled with screaming, yelling, and banging. Dylan's anxiety rises as the elongated halls narrow and the lights flicker on the stale gray walls. Dylan whispers to Dr. Roberts,

"Where are you taking me?"

Dr. Roberts rests her hand on Dylan's shoulders, leans toward her, and speaks quietly.

"Just to my office. It may be on skid row, but it is more comfortable than your room. Besides, I think you'll open up better in there."

Dr. Roberts opens her office door and inside is a plush lounge in heaven. The walls are lavender and violet. There are bright yellow curtains, a red chaise by the window, and yellow, orange, red, green, and purple accents everywhere. Dylan instantly feels drawn to the red chaise.

"Do I get to sit there? I'd prefer that chair instead of this handicapped ride."

Dr. Roberts smiles.

"Well…only if you promise to cooperate."

Dylan plops onto the red chaise beside the naked, full-length window. For a still moment she forgets she's under medical supervision as she focuses on a couple of birds flying in and out of an oak tree, splashing through a large puddle of water to clean their wings. She notices the distance from the window to the street is only two stories.

A loud scream echoes through the opening space under the office door, returning Dylan's focus to Dr. Roberts. Dylan laughs slyly, and speaks.

"So what do you want to know?"

Dr. Roberts smiles at Dylan, flips through her chart, and responds,

"Let's talk about your life at home."

Dylan responds with rude intent,

"Let's not."

Dr. Roberts returns with a stern command.

"No…let's. The sooner I know where the problem lies, the sooner you can go home."

Dylan temporarily submits, and entices Dr. Roberts's mind with a brief backstory.

"It's just me and my sister. No brothers. My dad's a cop and my mom's a semiretired OBGYN. Nothing special."

Dr. Roberts asks intensely,

"So are you happy? Do you get what you want in life? Are you spoiled?"

Dylan shifts her hips to dig deeper into the chaise.

"Happy…I guess. I guess I get what I want when I ask. Don't think I'm spoiled though…I mean, maybe, but shouldn't the baby of the family be spoiled?"

Dr. Roberts's eyebrows rise slightly. Dylan continues,

"I wouldn't say I'm really spoiled. I think my father just makes sure I feel loved...I mean, he shows me that I am loved. My mom and I aren't close really, and my sister...well, she despises the ground I float on. I guess my father's love for me bunches her feathers."

Dr. Roberts's eyes widen as if Dylan is approaching a break-through. She asks,

"Does your father show your sister the same kind of love?"

Dylan pauses briefly, looking into the air as if she's trying to recall affectionate episodes between her father and Janay. Dylan continues,

"I don't know. I think they aren't as close as he and I are. I think she wants his blessing in every aspect of her life, but she disappoints him in her actions toward me...I don't know. I know he loves her. I think he just wants her to love me. She hates me."

Dylan's eyes begin to water. She touches her forehead and rubs the side of her face. She continues,

"She displays her sisterly love through busted lips and black eyes. As long as I can remember, I've been fighting my way to get away from her. I remember being held under water in the bathtub when I was thirteen...now I can hold my breath for three minutes. I probably will be able to survive a kidnapping if someone tied me up and threw me off the pier...that is, if my feet aren't cemented."

Dylan laughs as her eyes fill with tears. Dr. Roberts looks at Dylan with empathy. She jots down a couple of notes, then places her pen down.

"Why do you think your sister has so much malice in her heart for you?"

Dylan shrugs her shoulders and looks out toward the window to see if the birds are still playing tag.

"I wonder if they are related. I would love to go to the beach and play with my sister. I guess that's life. Sibling rivalry...that's life too! At least I have Jazmine. She got my back...just like a real sister should. Those women are out to get me."

Dr. Roberts looks confused.

"I'm sorry, Dylan. Who's Jazmine, and what women are out to get you?"

Dylan laughs and says,

"They're supposed to protect me, especially Demi."

Dr. Roberts scratches her head and leans in closer to the chaise to follow Dylan's rant.

Dylan continues,

"It was a long time ago. Jazmine has always been by my side since we were young...like five years old. I'm really her only family. Her mother don't care much for her. She just loves to be loved by many men that she turns into stepfathers to love Jazmine. Anyway, she got my back and I got hers...though sometimes it seems like she has to have mine more than me having hers. But she's always there. She never really talks about the bumps and bruises she's endured. She only worries about mine. After all the bumps and bruises I've endured, I think my mind fought back and welcomed Demi. She's the other that helps me endure when I can't. My mother was supposed to protect me from my sister. But Demi does. She comes in with a vengeance. But the older I get, the less control I have over her. I don't know when she takes over, and I usually find out too late. She's like the best friend we love to hate, who always finds a way to buy the one thing you can't afford. If only I can rid myself of her, and all the other crazy women in my life."

Dr. Roberts is so intrigued, she writes frantically in her notes. She stands and begins walking in circles around the office while analyzing Dylan's words and experiences. She sits down at her desk and begins to fill out a prescription for Dylan.

She walks back to the chaise where Dylan sits wiping her eyes and staring out the window. Dr. Roberts sits on the edge of the chaise and speaks softly.

"Dylan, it's good you have a great friend like Jazmine. But I think right now our goal is to rid your mind of Demi and regain control over your body. Maybe one day you can be there for Jazmine too.

Dr. Roberts pauses...then continues,

"I think your loss of control of your alter is definitely a result of the stress you're under when faced with conflict with your sister. We have a lot of work to do. And it seems this alter, Demi, has been very busy...especially with the information your dad has given me."

Dr. Roberts picks up her office phone and calls for an orderly to pick up Dylan and take her back to her room.

She continues talking to Dylan.

"I'm not taking extreme measures now, so you'll go back to your room. The psych ward isn't going to be home for you just yet."

Chapter 10

HOME FOR THE HOLIDAYS

The next night after Dylan's arrival at the hospital, the food carts are stacked against the hallway corridor waiting for pickup from the cafeteria staff. The moans and frequent screams from connecting rooms begin to lessen as the reflective pain decreases with meds. Dylan settles in for her first night's stay as her bruises begin to darken with clotted blood. She replays the dark journey of her past and secrets with Dr. Roberts. Before her eyes can begin to water, she forces her eyes shut and settles in for a deep slumber.

Later, after the midnight hour, when creatures walk the earth in disarray, a shadow bounces off the gray walls of the hospital room, as the half-raised blinds present shimmers of car lights from the street. An aroma of musk and Jean Paul Gaultier filters the air, sending a mild breeze brushing past Dylan's eyelids. She turns slowly as her body awakens her from her slumber to face the doorway. She sees a pair of butter tan Timberland boots attached to the feet of a tall silhouette dressed in black. Dylan tries to close her eyes and return to her adventurous dreams of high-end shopping sprees, but her curiosity gets the best of her as she wonders who the Timberland boots belong to.

Dylan's eyes widen while scanning the room, searching for clues to confirm an orderly or male nurse was checking her vitals while she slept. Dylan notices a white rose tied to a newspaper clipping. She sits up and turns on the overhead light to observe the gift the anonymous figure left behind. As she unties the ribbon, the newspaper rolls open. Her eyes are instantly attracted to a bright pink Post-it note and a bold circle highlighting a want ad underneath. Dylan curiously reads the note out loud.

"I hear family put you here...perhaps moving out suits you best."

Dylan's curiosity keeps her awake throughout the night. Just as the sun begins to kiss the moon, Dylan's exhaustion takes the lead of her mind and places her body at rest.

Later in the morning, Dylan awakens to the sound of Dr. Roberts and her father talking between themselves, discussing alternative solutions for Dylan's twisted mind.

Dylan says with a groggy voice,

"Urghhhh! Ya'll can't whisper softly. I'm sleeping here. Dr. Roberts, can I go home now?"

Both the chief and doctor look at Dylan with concern. Chief Jones clears his voice and cuts the silence with authority.

"Hey, hey there, baby girl. Dr. Roberts brings good news. Be nice before she changes her mind."

Dylan rolls her eyes.

"Where's Ma?"

Chief Jones impatiently responds,

"You know where she is. That's not important now. What's important is that you will be home for Christmas..."

Dr. Roberts cuts in.

"But you have to come see me once every two weeks for status check-ins."

Dylan looks at Dr. Roberts and her dad and begins to giggle.

"Is that it? From the whispers and giggles, I thought ya'll were trying to hook up."

Chief Jones chimes in, and he looks Dr. Roberts up and down from head to toe.

"Dylan, that's enough. We both agree that with these check-ins and Dr. Roberts's treatment, you should be in the clear from the sticky situation you've been exposed to with Demi and the drama in West Virginia. You gotta stick to it for the heat to cool off...understand?"

Dylan innocently bats her curly lashes at Chief Jones before responding. She speaks softly and childlike.

"Yes, Daddy."

Chief Jones looks at Dylan and then at Dr. Roberts. He speaks with a lowered tone.

"We want what's best for you...we all do."

Dr. Roberts doesn't speak, but pulls her prescription pad out instead. She scribbles hastily and then quickly rips the script off the pad. She straightens her medical coat and says sternly,

"Patients first...that's my motto. I'll see you in two weeks after the first of the New Year. I hope you both have a Merry Christmas."

Dr. Roberts tightly pulls her lips apart from her teeth and smiles forcefully as she exits the room. She turns and gives Chief Jones a once-over look and winks.

Chief Jones smiles, rubs his beard, and winks at Dylan.

"It must be the uniform, baby girl...it always has that effect on women."

Dylan smiles and looks at her dad while shaking her head.

"Come on, Daddy, take me home."

Dylan sits in the passenger seat of her father's cruiser. She has flashes of her childhood and the embarrassment she used to feel when her dad would pick her up from school in the squad car. She smiled as she reminisced about not wanting the other kids to think she was being arrested. As she began to return to her present state of being, she notices her father is talking on his cell phone. Chief Jones pulls into the parking lot of the CVS pharmacy so he can get Dylan's prescription filled.

"Sweetie, do you want something from here?

Dylan looks over at her dad and smiles.

"Yes, some salt and vinegar chips and a Pepsi?

Before Chief Jones steps out of his cruiser, Dylan grabs his hand and says sweetly,

"Daddy, I really love you. Thank you for being there for me even when I disappoint you."

Chief Jones looks surprised, kisses Dylan's hand, and says,

"I love you too, sweetheart, unconditionally. There's nothing on this earth you could do to change that. I got you. No more worries."

Dylan closes her eyes to breathe in the cold fresh air while her dad is inside the store. She realizes after a while she is still gripping the newspaper that she found the night before in her hospital room. She unrolls the paper again and tries to figure out whether Big Rob paid her a visit or if Ray was trying to find his way back in her good graces. Just as she thinks more about it, Chief Jones is walking out of the store with a well-groomed police officer of lower rank. Dylan can't help but notice the tall man's bowlegs through his uniform pants. Just as she stares more intensely at his legs, making her way up toward his waist, she realizes the two men are standing in front of the cruiser speaking to her. Dylan's ear catches the last few words her father speaks as he repeats her name.

"Dylan…Dylan, I'd like you to meet Sergeant Foster, Sgt. Eric Foster.

Embarrassed yet slightly aroused, Dylan looks Sergeant Foster directly in the eyes, catching a glimpse of his hazel-grayish-brown pupils. She hides the hospital bracelet on her right hand with the newspaper and reaches outward with her left hand to respectfully greet the handsome figure.

She speaks shyly, allowing her hair to fall into her eyes.

"Hi, nice to meet you, Sergeant Foster."

Sergeant Foster smiles at Dylan and speaks with a deep voice like her dad's.

"Nice to meet you, beautiful. You can call me Eric."

The two men turn to continue talking with Chief Jones's back to Dylan. Sergeant Foster is looking over Chief Jones's shoulder, staring at Dylan as the two wrap up the conversation. Chief Jones hands Sergeant Foster an envelope and shakes his hand. Before Chief Jones enters the cruiser, he utters to Sergeant Foster,

"Do it fast...like yesterday."

Sergeant Foster winks at Dylan, puts his shades on, and walks away. Chief Jones gets into the car, noticing the intense attraction Dylan has for Sergeant Foster. He looks at Dylan and says jokingly,

"He's cute, isn't he? He's single too!"

Dylan smiles at her dad and says,

"What do you mean too? I'm sort of...well...whatever."

Chief Jones smiles at Dylan again and says,

"I think it would be good for you to meet a different class of people. Blue collars with pensions, and not deadbeat hustlers without insurance."

Dylan's semi-good attitude shifts drastically.

"Really, Dad. You haven't learned yet that I like bad boys or boys you despise. So telling me you found someone good for me is like writing a "not-to-date list.""

Chief Jones stares at Dylan blankly, and he realizes he probably blew the opportunity to spark interest between his daughter and his prodigy. Dylan leans back on the seat and stares out the window with a raised eyebrow, thinking to herself... Sergeant Foster could possibly be an exception.

Chapter 11

TRUE CONFESSIONS

The sunset halos across the barren trees, and a dull silence envelops the neighborhood homes. Chief Jones pulls his light blue Grand Marquis into the driveway of the Joneses' estate. He shuts the engine off, grabs Dylan's hand, and rubs it in a comforting way. He projects a sensitive voice.

"Baby girl, you know I love you, right?

Dylan turns and looks at her dad and wonders why the dramatic testimony.

"Of course I know you love me...but what's wrong now?"

Chief Jones stares at the front door of his home and looks back at Dylan with concern.

"I'm just concerned for your mental strength. The last time you were home, you were dragged away like a criminal."

Dylan frowns and understands the concern.

"I'm fine, Daddy. I'm just gonna go to my room and sleep. Deal with life tomorrow."

Chief Jones looks back at the front door and sighs briefly.

"OK, let's go. I'm guessing your mom will fuss over you to make sure you're OK...feed you, stuff you with dessert, and go back to her computer games."

Dylan laughs loudly and raises her eyebrow.

"I see a few days away from the homestead hasn't changed anything at all. I'll play nice. I promise."

The father-daughter duo exits the cruiser and heads up to the front door. Before Chief Jones can insert his key into the keyhole, the door springs open. Carmen stands in the doorway with her bathrobe on, wearing a pair of tennis shoes, and puffing on a cigarette that needs to be tapped to rid the ashes. Her eyes widen as Dylan appears beside Chief Jones.

"Oh, honey, I'm so glad you're home from the crazy house. Are you OK? Did anyone try to overpower you in there?"

Annoyed with her appearance, Chief Jones gently moves Carmen to the side.

"Enough with the twenty-one questions. Let baby girl get over the threshold before you bombard her. She's been through quite an ordeal."

Carmen taps the cigarette over Chief Jones's shoulder and rushes past the two, returning to her computer in the kitchen. She looks at Chef Jones, rolls her eyes, and lights another cigarette.

Dylan walks up the stairs to retreat to her bedroom. Just as she plops onto her bed, her bedroom phone rings. She leans over to catch a glimpse of the caller ID to see if she feels like talking. She answers.

"Hello...hey, Jaz, what's up?"

Jazmine's screeching voice seeps through the handset. Dylan continues,

"What? You've been worried about me. I know the last time we talked, I was going out with Ray. There's so much I need to tell you about Ray...yes, we are off again...I think. I mean, yes."

Dylan pauses as she reminisces about the warehouse and their rough sex, and then Big Rob. She continues,

"Where are you? Wait where? Oh, Dino...you haven't mentioned him in a while."

Jazmine blabbers nonstop for about thirty minutes about Dino, and Dylan listens intensely in between zoning out, recalling her horrific experiences in West Virginia and about her run in with Ray and Big Rob. Dylan comes back from her daze as she hears her cell phone buzzing. She searches around the room. She discovers it is lying under her dresser. She whispers over the top of Jazmine's chatter.

"So that's where you've been.

Jazmine pauses, then continues spewing about her tainted love for Dino and his drugs. Dylan reads the screen to her cell phone and discovers she has eighty-nine text messages from Jazmine, Big Rob, and Ray. She skims through the bulk of Jazmine's, which all have the same context... *Where are you?*

She continues skimming through, reading Ray's text messages professing his love for her. She's too scared to read Big Rob's. Her eyes catch a glimpse of one of his texts that reads,

Sorry for your fucked-up family. I hear they checked you in to the psych ward. I think it is best you move. Too much hovering will detonate my plans.

Her heart starts racing. She reads another one.

That pussy got me dreaming all kinds of bad things. Woke up with wet drawers last night.

She continues reading as she simultaneously hears Jazmine screaming through the phone.

Saw you in your hospital gown. Even in your sleep that pussy yearns for me. I hope you like the rose. Get an appointment to see that apartment I circled for you.

Dylan zones in on Jazmine's distress for attention.

"Jaz, let me call you back. Or better yet, come over. We need to talk."

Jazmine agrees to visit and hangs up the phone. Dylan goes to her bed and retrieves the newspaper that she found in her hospital room. Her heart races uncontrollably. She reads the circled newspaper ad.

Fun, Outgoing, Rock 'n' Roll, Music-Loving, Party-Going Female looking for a Fun, Outgoing, Rock 'n' Roll, Music-Loving, Party-Going roommate who loves designer shoes.

Twenty minutes later, Dylan is stepping out of the shower, drying off her caramel butter skin, staring into the mirror. She zones out and tears up as she has fragmented flashes of Ray's pathetic expression as Big Rob raped her. She begins crying harder. A knock on her bedroom door interrupts her crying session. It's her best friend, Jazmine. She opens the door and her blondish-orange tresses enter the bedroom first. She's dressed in all black with a royal green leather motorcycle jacket. Her joyful welcome delights Dylan,

"Bitch, put that crying gremlin away. We ain't lying down and being pussies."

She slams the bedroom door and hugs Dylan. She continues,

"I be damned if my girl is going to sit in this room and wallow and drown in her salty-ass tears. Get some clothes on, and let's blow this joint."

She opens her jacket and pulls out a stash of weed.

"I mean literally."

The two girls laugh briefly. Dylan walks Jazmine to her walk-in closet and closes the door. She pulls out two short stools for the two of them to sit for the storytelling session. Jazmine pulls out the pack of rice paper and starts rolling up fat joints.

Dylan raises her eyebrows.

"Jaz, what are you doing? I can't do that no more. I promised him."

Jazmine, unimpressed with Dylan's good-girl antics, replies,

"Who the chief? He ain't even here. Besides, how he going to let his wife smoke and not you? I know your mom be getting it in.

This good-girl facade you playing ain't working. Where's my old D? I know she's in there."

Jazmine fakes like she's knocking on Dylan's forehead.

Dylan's annoyance grows fast.

"All right, all right…just put a towel under the door and light some incense."

Dylan sits on the stool and reveals all the drama that she's endured.

"Ray set me up. When I talked to you the other day, we were headed out for an afternoon drive. That drive turned into some rough sex in a warehouse that he's using as a shoe business for a front to distribute massive drugs. We were interrupted by his crazy-ass brother who ended up tying me up, raping me, and knocking me over the head when I tried to get away. I woke up in some hick town jail cell with only a shirt. Clearly the fucking pricks should've have known that I was raped and needed medical attention. But no, they kept me locked in this jail cell. Oh…and I forgot to mention. Demi's back."

Jazmine pulls in a long drag.

"Really. I like Demi."

Dylan stares blankly at Jazmine.

"Shut up, ass. Demi needs to stay away, because she's got me into a whole lot of trouble. So let me finish."

Dylan takes the joint from Jazmine, inhales, coughs, and continues.

"So I wake up in the back of the rapist's truck. Apparently he came and rescued me in the nick of time as the fucking cops were trying to rape me. He tells me that I rocked the punk-ass cop so bad that his army of thugs torched the place to hide the evidence. Of course I'm shocked, because I don't remember anything, and at the same time he's telling me this, he's also threatening me to follow his instructions of bringing my father to his knees for some shit he did to him in the past."

Jazmine, now confused, tries to follow.

"So wait, if you don't remember beating up the cop, who did?

Dylan stares blankly at Jazmine.

"Are you serious? Were you even listening to me? Demi beat up the cops. She's back. Taking over my life. So he drops me off here...you hear me...here of all places. He knew where I lived. He and Ray have made friends with security, and they let them come and go as they please. So Big Rob is forcing me to follow his lead and is holding me hostage sort of. He says if I don't play by his rules, he will bring my father down...and may even kill him."

Jazmine asks curiously,

"Why don't you just tell your father everything?"

Dylan responds,

"Ashamed of all I went through...because I sort of enjoyed it. Not being raped and being forced—but I have to admit, the sex was good in a sense. Better than Ray even. All I think about is the night I met Ray. I told you he wasn't aggressive enough, and he was probably driving his uncle's truck...well it was actually his brother's. My intuition was right."

Jazmine laughs.

"You know, the old heads always say trust your intuition.

Dylan smiles.

"I know. So let me finish. Janay is on my ass, which is how I ended up in the hospital."

Jazmine starts flaring her nostrils as she grows angry.

"That bitch. She just needs one good ass whooping. I'll do it. You know I will."

Dylan grins at her best friend's allegiance.

"I know. So she's hell-bent on turning me in for the West Virginia stuff…even though I didn't kill anyone. And to make things worse, I have to see a psychiatrist now. Remember that doctor we were talking to in my mother's office? She's my new shrink. She's cool. Dr. Roberts. Anyway, you are the only one I've told all of this to. I didn't even speak of the events to Dr. Roberts. Not even the rape."

Jazmine's eyes water as she speaks.

"So what are you gonna do?"

Dylan gives Jazmine a warm, pathetic look. She bats her eyes.

"I just need you to be there for me. Even when I'm crazy or weak and Demi surfaces. But as long as I take this new prescription, I should be good."

Jazmine smiles.

"I got your back, D…you my girl. Ain't nobody gonna fuck with you again. Not on my watch."

The girls hug and continue smoking their weed. Dylan remembers one last thought. She continues,

"So Big Rob has been texting me, trying to get me from under this roof. He brought this newspaper ad to my hospital room."

She hands Jazmine her cell phone to let her read the text messages, and then hands her the newspaper ad. Jazmine reads silently for a few minutes.

Jazmine smiles through her analytical thoughts.

"He's quite intriguing. I think I understand why you are confused. Hell, I wish he was texting me. Damn. Well, maybe we should call and find out about the ad. Maybe moving out of this house can help you turn the tables on Big Rob and bring him down. He won't see it coming."

The girls laugh and hug. Dylan grabs a can of the aerosol Lysol and sprays the closet down. She glares at the FSW shoe boxes in the corner. She shuts her eyes in a haste to forget about Ray.

Jazmine starts rummaging through the clothes in the closet. Dylan looks at her watch lying on the counter.

"Do you think it's too late to call? It's only ten o'clock."

Jazmine looks back at Dylan. Stop your worrying. We'll call tomorrow. Right now, I gotta feed the beast in my belly."

Dylan looks stumped and glares back at Jazmine.

"Actually, I'm hungry too. Let's see what Carmen whipped up."

Chapter 12

FUN, OUTGOING, ROCK 'N' ROLL, MUSIC-LOVING, PARTY-GOING DESIGNER SHOE LOVER

The blistering cold front, projected by Tipper Brown on Fox Five News, blusters through the sleeping neighborhoods, leaving thick winds and weightless falling snow. Jazmine wakes up to the smell of roasted beans brewing in the Keurig coffee maker downstairs in the kitchen. She jumps up in a haste trying to make sense of her surroundings. She notices Dylan sleeping on the bed with her robe on. Jazmine grabs the newspaper ad once more and reassures herself that moving out is the best thing for Dylan.

The sound of Carmen's voice shakes Dylan out of her sleep. She stretches and yawns. She sits up and notices Jazmine lying on the floor with her legs in the air.

"Crazy, what the hell are you doing?"

Jazmine lifts her head up.

"I am semi exercising. A few leg lifts before the morning strut deployment works well for my figure."

The girls stare each other and then burst out laughing.

"Jaz, I've missed you. I'm glad you came over last night. You're the sister I should've had."

Jazmine gives Dylan a hug and smiles. She speaks softly.

"I know D…don't get so sappy. Let's get this show on the road. Call about the ad in the paper."

Dylan stands up and walks to her bathroom. She washes her face and brushes her teeth. When she returns to her indented space on her bed, her cell phone chimes off a text message alert.

Jazmine sits up straight.

"Who is it? Is it Mr. Rob?

Dylan says with frustration,

"His name is Big Rob…not mister. He is not my master."

Jazmine frowns at her.

Dylan reads the screen of her cell phone out loud.

"Look, you cunt…my patience is running low. Make the call, meet your roommate, and get out from under that psycho roof. You have three days. Noon today, meet me at Club Red. You'll be starting your new job."

Dylan is frozen. Jazmine grabs the phone and reads the message for herself.

"Yo…dude is psycho. Who does he think he is? I think we need to go to your father."

Dylan's shell is frozen. Her eyes darken and her lashes bat sporadically. Demi awakes. She stands up and stretches. She notices Jazmine sitting on the floor staring at her.

"Awwwwe shit…the flower child is here to visit."

Jazmine is surprised my Demi's appearance. She holds her cell phone up and snaps a picture of Demi and says excitedly,

"OMG, Demi. I can't believe it."

Demi looks at Jazmine and her eyes widen.

"Well believe it, baby. I couldn't take all the fucking croco-dile tears. Lil' Ms. Goodie Princess is too weak. Gotta land this plane before the infamous crash landing."

Demi looks at the bathrobe and laughs.

"What is she doing to this body? I know she's not taking fash-ion tips from Carmen."

Jazmine laughs out loud.

"Yo...you are funny as shit. I can't stop laughing."

Demi looks around. She grabs the phone from Jazmine.

"Is this what got her panties in a bunch? I can handle this fucker. Let's call this chick in the newspaper first. I can play by his rules, 'cause a bitch is trying to get that dick again. Mhmmmm! That shit was off the chain."

Jazmine is so intrigued by Demi, she sits with her mouth hanging open.

"I fucks with you, Demi. I can roll with that."

Demi grabs the paper and dials the number listed in the ad.

"Hi, is dis the '*Fun, Outgoing, Rock 'n' Roll, Music-Loving, Party-Going Female that loves Designer Shoes?*...Mmhmmm! Today's good...OK, I'll see you at six o'clock."

Demi looks at Jazmine and smiles.

"Check. That's off the list. Now we gotta go meet this punk-ass Big Rob. Let's grab something to eat and roll out this bitch."

Demi walks into the bathroom with a pill bottle in her hand. She opens the top and pours the pills into the toilet.

"In order for me to save you from yourself, this is the way it has to be...maybe forever."

Demi meets Jazmine downstairs in the kitchen. She over-hears Jazmine making small talk with Carmen. Demi looks at Carmen, rolls her eyes, and motions for Jazmine to follow.

"Hi, Carmen...what's up?"

Carmen immediately recognizes the familiar tone. She grabs her cigarette pouch.

"Oh...I thought they got rid of you."

Demi stares at Carmen as Jazmine walks over and gives Carmen a hug. Demi says, "Oh, sorry, old lady...though pleasing you isn't high on my list, I will be leaving here for good... sooner than you imagine."

Carmen is shocked for the back talk. She begins coughing as she lights up her cigarette.

"What do you mean, leaving here for good? You can't leave...I mean Dylan can't leave. Her dad won't stand for it."

Demi looks at Jazmine, and motions her to follow her to the front door.

"Come on, Jazmine, gotta make some moves."

Carmen starts yelling and screaming.

"Jazmine, did you see her medicine? She has to take her medicine."

Demi laughs wickedly as the two head out the front door.

"Jazmine, I got this. No need to worry about her shenanigans."

Demi follows Jazmine to her car.

"I can't believe your girl crashed up her car. I hear Big Pop is supposed to be footing an SUV bill for her."

ᴄᴏ

The two girls pull up in Jazmine's Honda Accord in front of Club Red. Jazmine looks around.

"How will we know who Big Rob is?"

Demi swipes Jazmine on the forehead.

"Duh...you think I wouldn't remember that ass if I saw it? Matter fact, I can't wait to see it."

They step out of the car. Demi stops Jazmine at the door. She looks her up and down and straightens her clothes. Demi says,

"I gotta take care of you too?"

Demi notices Jazmine is wearing the fingerless black knit glove.

"How you trying to be gothic with these fuck 'em pumps on?"

Jazmine remains silent.

Demi grabs Jazmine's hand and says,

"What are you hiding under here?"

Jazmine yanks her hand away.

Demi stares blankly and says with annoyance,

"I'm not trying to get in your business. I guess I gotta look out for you too...I gotta save the world."

Jazmine stands frozen and then snaps out of her zone quickly as Demi opens the doors to the club. The interior walls of the club entrance are covered in red stones, with white marble ceilings and red leather seating. There are mirrors all over the walls on each side of the club, with a large chandelier elevated over the center of the white marble dance floor. Demi walks in, and she starts gyrating as if she's revving up her hips for a night of vaginal satisfaction. The girls are drawn to look above their heads to a wide balcony overlooking the entrance to the club. They start walking up the stairs toward the overlook. Demi stops abruptly when they reach the top of the stairs. She spots Big Rob standing up against the bar holding a brandy glass and sipping simultaneously as he rocks to the rhythm of the bass being projected from the surround sound.

Demi looks him straight in the eyes.

"You summoned me..."

Big Rob walks over to her and starts dry humping the space in between the two of them.

"I thought you'd disobey and force me to discipline you."

He leans in toward her. Jazmine interjects by extending her hand toward him.

"Hi...I'm Jazmine. The best friend. The gatekeeper. What do you want with my girl?"

Big Rob halts his perverted display of affection and stares Jazmine directly in her face.

"I'm sorry...don't think I invited you to this reunion. Dylan, who do we have here?"

Demi annoyingly looks at Big Rob.

"Let's get something straight. My name is Demi. I keep telling you this. Secondly, this is my homegirl Jazmine. She's harmless. She's like my personal bodyguard."

Big Rob looks Jazmine up and down. Walks behind her and checks out her rack and her backseat.

"Mmmmmm. OK. I might have room for one more. There's always room on a stripper pole."

Jazmine screeches loudly.

"What the hell. Who you think you pimping? I'm just here with my girl 'cause we got stuff to do."

Big Rob smiles.

"Well, Ms. Demi is going to be pretty busy today.

He walks toward Demi, guides her by the waist, and walks her down the stairs.

"I know you ain't used to this life, but you might like it. I think I'm gonna start you off downstairs until you warm up."

He walks her to the large bar on the first level of the club.

"Do you know how to bartend?"

Jazmine follows behind them. Before Demi can speak up, Jazmine answers,

"We know how to drink cocktails...so I'm sure we can figure out how to mix them."

Big Rob turns to Jazmine.

"It sounds like you're back on board."

Demi turns to Big Rob.

"I can swing this. I'm not shy around the bottle or the atmosphere...but what's the catch?"

Big Rob strokes his goatee, licks his lips, and says,

"You know our deal. You let me turn you out, change that good-girl image to bad, and your daddy stays in the clear. Do what I say, for as long as I say, and we're good."

Demi smiles slyly, looks over at Jazmine, and winks.

Big Rob looks at both girls.

"Looks like double trouble to me...I might have to rethink this."

Jazmine winks at Big Rob and says,

"Look, I'm down for the fun, but if you didn't know, some nights we...well, our band plays around the city."

Rob strokes his goatee.

"No worries. Let's call this home base. Just gather new clientele and bring them back here. It will work for everyone."

Jazmine looks at her watch. She screeches.

"Demi...we gotta go. Big Rob, I hate to leave all this fun, but if you want your girl to make her appointment for the apartment...we must leave now."

Demi walks from behind the bar, grabs Big Rob's hand, and leads him to the back of the club to the ladies' restroom. She throws him on the sofa in the lounge area and sits on top of him.

Big Rob smiles.

"Oh, what's this? I see you haven't asked about my lil' brother. Does this mean you've accepted me?"

Demi smiles.

"Listen, that punk Ray is dead to me. I need an alpha male."

Big Rob starts kissing Demi. She stops him in his tracks.

"Look, how long is this going to last? I think I could be down with all of this without my hands being tied."

She begins unzipping his pants. She whispers in his ear, "What do you really want from me?"

He flips her over, pulls her pants down, and forces one leg out. He rips her panties off. He pulls her hips upward and rubs her butt, outlining the shape.

"I see you missed me as much as much as I missed this wet pussy."

Demi lifts her head up.

"I got your text. You've been dreaming about me…huh?"

Big Rob rams his junk in her cookie jar as far as it can go. Her head bounces off the wall in a rhythmic motion. He releases inside her, and she breathes hard like a cat in heat. Demi moans and pushes him off her and forces him on his back. She sits on top of him and takes the reigns as if she's riding Black Beauty in the Kentucky Derby. Big Rob's mouth is wide open in disbelief. He's lost control of the enemy and realizes she's not such a goody-goody after all.

When Demi climaxes, she stands up and lets all their juices dangle from her forest of love. She catches a glimpse of a decent smirk on Big Rob's face, as if he's been turned. She pulls her pants up, straightens her hair, and walks out of the bathroom, leaving Big Rob vulnerable and shriveled up.

Demi returns to the front of the club and finds Jazmine laughing and throwing back shots with the bouncers.

Demi walks to the door and grabs a joint out of a bouncer's hand. She puffs and pulls in a long drag. She coughs.

"'Ey, flower child. Let's go! There's an apartment with my name on it."

The two chicks head to the parking lot. Demi demands the keys from Jazmine.

"I'll drive."

Demi peels out of the parking lot, leaving skid marks and a cloud of marijuana smoke behind them.

The modern lampposts and intricately cultivated landscapes outline the perimeter of the gated condo community in southeast Washington, DC. The sign, encased by brick and stone, reads, Chesapeake Condos.

Jazmine and Demi walk up to the building with the same address as the one in the ad, eight hundred Chesapeake Street SE, Washington, DC. Jazmine pushes the button for suite number eight. The girls wait patiently. Demi pushes the button again.

The static from the intercom interrupts the girls' patience. A voice chimes through.

"Yes, can I help you?"

Demi nonchalantly replies,

"Kennedy, it's me...Demi. We spoke this morning. I'm interested in your room to rent."

Kennedy excitedly responds,

"Excellent...let me buzz you in!"

Kennedy greets Demi at her door. Her long blond bob cut bounces in and out of place. Her bangs flow back and forth as she jumps up in excitement.

"Hi, there. Welcome!"

Kennedy looks at Jazmine and Demi. She is trying to figure out which one is Demi. She looks down at Demi's black studded peep-toe shoe boot.

"Hi, you must be Demi! I am loving your shoes. Your style tells me we are definitely pegged to be roommates. Come on in!"

Demi and Jazmine walk across the threshold of Kennedy's condo. They look at each other and nod in sequence with agreement every so often as Kennedy gives the grand tour to her palace. She shows the girls three empty rooms, including her own, which has wall-to-wall shelves attached to the walls with high heels residing across the whole room.

Kennedy says,

"I know the ad specified a room for rent, but as you can see, there is more than enough room for two renters."

Jazmine smiles.

"I'm just here to support my girl. I need a good job first before I jump out of my mother's nest."

Demi looks through the condo and stands in place. She nonchalantly admires the digs, and says,

"It's not the palace I'm used to, but this place is beautiful."

Kennedy smiles with excitement.

"Can you see yourself living here?"

Demi smiles cunningly.

"I sure can! So…what size shoe do you wear?"

Kennedy answers with caution,

"I'm a size seven and a half on a good day, when I'm not mixing drinks all day. Why do you ask?"

Demi jokingly smiles.

"Just don't want my stockpile of shoes to be kidnapped."

Kennedy laughs.

"I won't kidnap yours if don't kidnap mine! Are you a shoe whore like me?"

Demi laughs hysterically,

"Word is…I'll do anything or anyone, for an unlimited supply of shoes."

Kennedy smiles with shock.

"Girlfriend…I think we're twins, switched at birth."

Demi winks.

"Well then, darling…I'm in."

Jazmine breaks the mold.

"Thank God! This was getting awkward. I thought you two were about to slob each other down."

Demi looks at Jazmine.

"Shut up, flower child."

Kennedy, confused about the inside joke, continues,

"So, twin, your first and last month's rent has already been taken care of."

Shocked and confused, Demi responds,

"What? By who?"

Jazmine walks toward the newfound twins and puts her hands around Demi's neck and fakes, like she's choking a pound of sense into her brain,

"Are you seriously going to stand here and act shocked?"

Demi pauses for a moment while her frontal lobe downloads common sense...

"How do you know Big Rob? Is this another one of his setups?"

Kennedy chimes in her response.

"I'm not certain or aware of a setup. I'm not a cop...I'm a dancer at Club Red. Big Rob and I go way back. He's good people. He looks out for me. In my former life, I used to date his brother, but he couldn't handle me. Anyway, I've been looking out for Big Rob for years. He's like my big brother.

Kennedy stares at Demi with curiosity.

"So how do you know him?"

Demi rolls her eyes at Kennedy.

"I really..."

Jazmine interrupts.

"Girl, he's sweet on her. Since she's trying to escape her dad's protective barrier, I guess he thought your ad would be a good start for my girl's escape."

Demi's bewildered attitude goes right over the bubbly condo owner's excitement. Kennedy smiles at the duo and says,

"Well, just let me know what you want to do. As you can see, I have more than enough room."

Jazmine and Demi walk to the door together. Demi looks back as she opens the door.

"I'll let you know. Thanks for the tour, Kennedy."

Chapter 13

PILLOW TALK

Two days before Christmas engulfs the atmosphere of suburban Maryland. A fresh coat of white snow blankets the neighborhood where the Joneses sleep. Jonathan Jones awakens to the sound of Carmen's cell phone buzzing. Before he opens his eyes, Carmen leans over and grabs the phone from her nightstand. She glances at the first few lines of the text,

"Just arrived. Hoping I could see you for old times' sake. Call..."

Carmen closes out the screen nervously.

Jonathan grunts.

"Who the hell is buzzing you at four in the morning, Mrs. Jones...aren't you on sabbatical?"

She lays the phone on her nightstand. She clears her throat and says,

"Just a patient who wants a home visit."

Jonathan lies still and responds,

"There is a time and place for business, and home is where you rest."

Carmen smiles, as she appreciates Jonathan's no-nonsense attitude about mixing business and pleasure.

"Yes, honey, I gotcha."

Carmen rolls over to face Jonathan to take advantage of the time to gain some pillow talk.

She pulls her nightgown over her head and sits on top of Jonathan. He opens his eyes.

"Ohhh! You're feeling frisky."

Carmen unleashes her swinging monkeys from the clasps of her bra. She pulls Jonathan's plaid pajama pants down.

"I see he's not awake."

Jonathan clears his throat,

"Well, wake him up."

Carmen throws her head back in preparation. She does a few throat exercises and tunes her vocal cords. She slides down his trunk and sucks the ash off his skin.

Jonathan moans and reaches for Carmen's head. Her wig accidently gets caught in his jagged fingernail. He flings it off and it lands on top of the lampshade. Jonathan taps Carmen's butt giving her the cue to climb back on top of him. She lands her gear right on the erect bull's-eye, guiding the missile to the hot spot. Carmen bellows out a graceful chord and rolls off Jonathan.

"Early morning glory...gotta love it."

Jonathan rolls over on top of her and takes his pitch to the final inning. He pants like an aging gorilla.

Two minutes later, he's drifting into a deep slumber. Carmen interjects the post celebratory rest. She shakes his chest.

He responds hoarsely,

"Yes, dear."

Carmen sighs.

"I've been meaning to talk to you about Dylan. She's checked out. Demi is on the prowl."

"This can't be. The doctor prescribed her a new medicine to keep Demi away."

Jonathan gets antsy and attempts to sit up in the bed. Carmen grabs his chest and softly calms him.

"Honey, relax. I've figured it out...Demi is the protector when she's stressed. We gotta let it ride for a while. Then this too shall pass."

Jonathan sighs.

"It's just not normal. Dylan and I just had a talk. She was talking about possibly signing up for the academy."

Carmen sighs.

"She will, honey. Just let time heal everything."

Jonathan breathes deeply for strength to survive the early morning conversation.

"We have to keep her closely monitored. I was thinking of getting her a new ride...that is only if she joins the academy.

Carmen sits up straight in the bed.

"A new car? What does she need a new car for?"

She sucks her teeth in a jealous rage, and continues spewing...

"You always reward her for nothing. Maybe that's where we went wrong with Janay. She was never spoiled like Dylan."

Jonathan grunts with annoyance.

"I promised her I would get her the SUV she's been talking about. She needs something reliable. Something better than the sedan she crashed in the ditch."

Carmen laughs sarcastically.

"That girl has you wrapped around her fingers. All of them. You never brought Janay a car."

Jonathan stares blankly at Carmen.

"Dear, not today, especially when the sun hasn't risen. Speaking of our eldest...have you heard from the rebel? She's mad at me since I suspended her."

Carmen frowns while pulling the covers over her droopy breasts.

"No, she's mad at me too. She's just evil. She has so much contempt for Dylan. You know we missed her birthday. It was the morning of the altercation where she dragged baby girl out of here."

Jonathan sighs.

"It's been this way since Dylan was born. Why are you acting surprised? She'll learn...probably real hard, but she'll learn."

Jonathan kisses his wife on the forehead and slumps farther down into the sheets. Carmen leans over to grab her favorite pouch of nicotine treats. She looks over at Jonathan and speaks with assurance.

"Things will get better. The holidays should mellow everything out. We're a few days from Christmas. Dylan loves this time of year...Speaking of this time of year, our anniversary is coming."

Jonathan sighs.

"Yes, dear...forty years. It's come so fast. Where has the time gone?"

Carmen smiles proudly.

"Well make sure your time is prioritized. Our anniversary party is less than two weeks away. Marrying you on New Year's Day was the craziest decision I ever made...but I wouldn't change anything about it. It was so special...it was the beginning of a revolution."

Jonathan coughs through Carmen's smoke.

"Yes dear, I agree. A revolution. Forty years of craziness."

Jonathan drifts off into a slumber.

Wide-eyed and bushy tailed, Carmen tries to spark a debate.

"What did you say? Jonathan...what did you say?"

After total fail, she finishes up the nicotine treat and lights up her special rolled stick filled with fresh crumbled herbs. Then she heads downstairs for an early breakfast.

Chapter 14

FRESHMAN ORIENTATION

The sound of grease bullets popping in the air from the frying bacon and the smell of rising pancake dough glides across the nostrils of Dylan's sleeping body. Her shell is stretched across the plush orange plaid sofa in the Joneses' living room. Her purple skinny jeans are halfway unzipped, extending space for her curvy hips and butt to seep over the back. Her black-and-white striped shirt has rolled up slightly above her rib cage. The sun reflects subtly on her auburn highlights as her tresses fall over her eyes. Her eyes pop open. Carmen notices a pair of arms stretched outward and hears a loud groan bellow out from beyond the couch.

Carmen walks over to the couch and leans over Dylan's body. She speaks cautiously.

"Dylan...wake up. Dylan."

Carmen reaches her hand to touch her shoulder.

"Dylan, are you hungry?"

The awakened beauty rolls over. Demi speaks,

"Urgghhh! What? Whatchu want, Carmen?"

Carmen is disappointed it is Demi who has been awakened.

"Excuse me? Let's get it straight—respect is still the rule around here. Now get up. Sleeping on my good couch. Where you been all night?"

Annoyed, Demi sits up and pulls her shirt down.

"None of your damn business. I'm grown."

Shocked and annoyed, Carmen says angrily,

"Look, Dylan, you and the disrespect will not be tolerated."

Demi chuckles sarcastically,

"Yo C...How many times we gotta rehearse this shit with you. I'm not Dylan. Repeat after me...DEEMEEEE."

Carmen stands up straight and walks toward the stairs.

"That's it. I've had enough. Your father will have to deal with you."

Demi chuckles in between imitating Carmen's frustration.

"'Ey, Carmen, where is the chief? We need to talk. I need some dough to get up outta here."

Twenty minutes later, Demi is sitting at the kitchen table wolfing down the scrambled eggs, bacon, fried potatoes, grits, and pancakes Carmen prepared in her marijuana-induced craving. Jonathan heads toward the kitchen with Carmen stomping in front of him. He glimpses at Demi's frivolous ingestion.

"Good morning, Demi."

Demi stops chewing and turns, quickly facing Jonathan.

"Chief...good morning. Glad you...we, understand each other. Carmen, you can take a few lessons from Chief. He knows my name. Learn it, rehearse it, live it."

Demi laughs in between chewing and drinking her juice.

"Look here...there was some talk about the purchase of a new car...a white GMC to be exact. Need to know when we can go grab it. Gotta lot of moves to make."

Jonathan grabs a plate off the counter and stockpiles his breakfast. He sits beside Demi.

"I certainly hope one of those moves is to sign up for the academy."

Demi pauses, staring into the air for three seconds.

"The academy…is that what she promised you?"

She pauses again.

"Maybe. That might be cool. Can you see me brandishing a pistol?"

Demi raises her hand up like she's pointing a gun at the aging couple.

"Freeze."

She chuckles loudly. Carmen sits down at the table. She opens a bottle of rum cream and pours it into her coffee mug.

Demi looks at Carmen with disgust.

"Life got you down? I guess its five o'clock somewhere."

Demi looks back at Jonathan.

"So, Chief, what about it…when can you grab that whip for me?

"As soon as Dylan returns and signs up for the academy. Gotta make sure responsibility is the path she's focused on. She's gotta start making her own money."

"Oh, that might be a problem. I don't think Dylan wants to come back. But I got you. I can handle the academy. But…I did grab a gig yesterday. I start today, as a matter of fact."

Jonathan scratches his head as he cautiously plays the ego game with Demi.

"Not another club to play at with the band?"

Demi smirks.

"The band…nawwww, that's D's thing. It's something better. But I might chip in here and there to play for her."

Demi starts gyrating at the table.

"The audience loves when I'm up there. I take over. I run the set."

Carmen jumps up.

"I can't take this. She has to go. She has to get out of here… this house. I can't take her anymore."

She walks over to her favorite spot in the kitchen. She sits down in front of her computer and zones out while her husband and his new daughter chat away with their nonsense.

Demi smirks with satisfaction.

"You know, Carmen doesn't miss a beat in trying to get rid of me. So maybe it will be best that I pack up Dylan's things and roll."

Jonathan takes a sip of his coffee.

"Move out...that's not necessary."

Demi continues,

"I think it's time. And my new gig and other opportunities will help pay the bills."

Demi leans in toward Jonathan and bats her eyes in a way that Dylan would to get what she wants. She continues,

"Of course I would need your financial support, Daddy."

Jonathan scratches his head in confusion. He momentarily thinks Dylan has reawakened. He suspects Demi is playing a strategic hand for a purpose. So in an attempt to play his cards right with Demi, and to hopefully reach Dylan's side of the brain, Jonathan continues stroking Demi's ego.

"Maybe the independence would be good for Dylan. It might give her exactly what she's lacking. Hopefully she can start taking her meds again...'cause I know she can't be medicated if you're here. With independence and confidence, she won't have to rely on you."

Demi pauses with caution. Her satisfaction increases.

"Really. OK. Maybe not the meds. But we might have a deal."

Jonathan smiles.

"Well, this is a beginning...I just had a thought. You and Carmen don't get along too well. But Dylan loves her. Maybe as a start to our new partnership...perhaps we could soften your relationship with Carmen by inviting you and the band to play at our anniversary party."

Demi pauses and breaks out in laughter.

"I ain't thinking about Carmen liking me. I think we get along just fine. But since I like you and I need that SUV, I'll consider."

Jonathan laughs at Demi's negotiation skills. He gets up from the table and heads toward the front door to leave for work. He kisses Carmen on the cheek.

"I'll think about it, Ms. Demi...but one thing at a time."

At the stroke of 7:00 p.m., Demi stands in the full-length mirror of Dylan's bedroom looking at her sexiness. She drapes herself in black leather shorts with a black fitted T-shirt with white lettering displaying *Club Red*. Demi outlines her eyes with smoky gray eyeliner and swipes a subtle layer of red eye shadow across her eyelids. She sprays a cloud of Seduction perfume across her neck and the back of her wrists. As she leans over to zip up the side zippers of her pointed-toe black leather knee boots, her cell phone buzzes an alert. She discovers Jazmine sent a text message, letting her know she was pulling up in front of the Joneses' estate. Demi leans toward the mirror so close that a misty fog appears on the mirror while she layers her lips with a matted red lipstick. She kisses the mirror and heads out the bedroom door to join Jazmine in her car to start their first day of skeptical labor at Club Red.

An all-black Chevy Impala with deep black tinted windows follows Jazmine's gold Honda once she exits the gated community. The Impala stays five cars behind to ensure it's not sighted by the girls.

A half hour later, the two twenty-year-old promiscuous girls enter the club and are drooled over by heavily aroused old, handicapped, educated, dyslexic, thin, fat, and bald men sitting at the bar. The dance floor is packed by eager, money-hungry girls who spend all their time swinging their weaves and checking their makeup in their handheld compacts while frowning at unwanted dance partners. Demi recognizes one of the bartenders from the impromptu interview the other day and leans over to say hello and to ask where she is assigned. He points upward, cuing her to go upstairs to see Big Rob. Jazmine stays behind to chat with the bartender, and Demi heads up the stairs. She sees Big Rob sitting at the bar with a bunch of women dancing around him. He motions for Demi to join them. She walks over to him and sits down at the bar. She turns to him and starts gyrating, directing his attention to only her. Big Rob snaps his fingers and the women disperse. Demi looks at him.

"So you want me to move in with Ray's old girlfriend?"

Big Rob smiles.

"Oh, so you went to see the apartment. Did you like it? You need to move quickly."

Demi pauses and responds,

"Well obviously it doesn't matter if I like it or not. You've already paid the deposit and rent. What if I don't do it?"

Big Rob stares at her with disappointment.

"You know what the consequences are."

Demi raises her voice and says,

"Are you really gonna keep saying you'll kill the chief? I do what I want. This is fun for me; it's not torture."

Big Rob smirks at her and turns away.

Demi realizes his obsession really isn't about the chief anymore.

"OK, so what you got on my agenda tonight? Am I showing titties, ass, or dancing?"

He grins.

"You are really a bad girl. Very eager to start your first day, huh?"

Demi smiles back.

"As eager as a stripper in a glittery pole store."

Big Rob laughs out loud.

"Slow down. You're right. I may have to rethink my strategy with you. You're too willing and not scared of what Daddy really thinks.

Demi smiles.

"Oh yeah. I'm off the hook? I'm free? No more blackmail? No more revenge? You letting the chief off too?"

Big Rob grabs his crotch...

"Hmmmm! You're not off the hook. Can't reveal my line of defense. If I tell you, I'll have to..."

He quickly swipes his index finger across his neck. Then he laughs loudly.

"I'm fucking wit' you. Can't let you off that easy. Let's see what the night brings. Right now, you and Jazmine can start your shift here at this bar."

As the night progresses, the girls handle the massive drink orders without stress. The music is pumping and the four miniature stages in the back corners hold an assortment of obese, anorexic, voluptuous, toned, cellulous thighs, butts, and breasts as dollars glide off the skin of the dancing bodies. Jazmine dances fast to the beat of the music while pouring drinks and making friends. Big Rob walks up to the bar with an empty glass.

"Refresh my drink, and then bring your sexy ass out here and show me your other talents."

Jazmine excitedly pours Big Rob another drink and walks from behind the bar. Big Rob escorts Jazmine to the left back corner stage.

"The nine o'clock shift didn't show. You're on."

Jazmine immediately starts dancing slowly. She bends over, allowing her leather miniskirt to rise. She attempts to swing around the pole and ends up with a harsh burn from the friction. As she continues her audition, a bright spotlight appears in the back right corner. A woman is dressed in a white-collared shirt, thigh-high fishnet stockings, and red stiletto pumps. The music slows as she performs, peeling off her white-collared shirt, leaving only her white thong on display. The long spiked blond bob falls in the woman's eyes. She swipes her tresses, clearing her vision.

Demi stands at the bar frozen as her eyes are drawn to the woman onstage. The crowd applauses nonstop after Kennedy's mini performance, and when the spotlight disappears, Demi realizes it's her potential new roommate, Kennedy. The two lock eyes, and Kennedy steps off stage. She heads toward the bar. Demi stands speechless as Kennedy sits in front of her and buttons her shirt.

"Hey, twin.

Demi smiles.

"Girl, you were hot. Got me over here questioning my sexuality."

Kennedy laughs.

Demi continues,

"I thought you said you bartended here."

Kennedy laughs, saying,

"I do. But you'll soon realize where the money lies... gotta go. Hope to see you at home soon."

Kennedy runs to the back, and Demi follows her.

"Wait, so everyone does everything here."

Kennedy goes into the locker room.

"Seems like you're interested."

Demi looks at Kennedy with curiosity.

"Maybe. I gotta plan. A one-month plan. Gotta make some moves."

Kennedy opens a closet in the locker room and reveals a closetful of outfits.

"Try it out. Maybe you can go save your girl, Jazmine."

Demi walks out dressed as a chambermaid. She steps onto the back left stage where Jazmine is struggling to hold herself up on the pole, boring Big Rob. Demi looks up at the DJ and cues him to play something fast. Jazmine's relieved look motivates Demi to outdo her.

The spotlight brightens on Demi, and she performs as if she is onstage with the Flaming Rejects. She gyrates, fondles herself, and undresses down to the black-laced thong. Big Rob gets aroused and throws his hands up for the spotlight to shut off. He pulls a small vial out of his pocket. He sprinkles a little white dust on the stretch of his thumb and pushes Demi's face toward it. Just as she leans in to submit and sniff it inside her flaring nostrils, a camera flashes in her face. Demi flinches as her mind struggles to shift back to Dylan. Her shell stands frozen. Rob turns away from her and searches the crowd for the cameraman. He notices a curvy figure, with a camouflage cap on, run down the stairs. He looks over the balcony and sees the back of the woman headed to the front of the club's entrance. On his way down the stairs to chase her, he sees his brother, Ray's, reflection in the mirror on the wall. He's sitting at the bar drinking. He bypasses Ray and rushes outside after the woman. Just as he rushes to the parking lot, a black Impala speeds past him and jumps the curb, peeling down the street.

Inside the club, Demi fights the transition of Dylan and begins to hallucinate. She laughs uncontrollably at flying images surrounding her. Jazmine runs over to Demi and shakes her shoulders, trying to get her eyes to focus.

"Demi, Demi...are you OK?"

Demi pauses, seeking confirmation that she fought off Dylan's return. She looks around the club. She swipes the rolling sweat beads dripping from her brow and down her temple. She looks at Jazmine with confusion.

"Flower child...what happened?"

Kennedy rushes over toward the girls and sits next to Jazmine. Kennedy high-fives them both, and she looks Demi directly in her eyes. She giggles.

"Welcome to the club, twin. Looks like at least one of you've passed freshmen orientation."

Chapter 15

BELLS WILL RING...

THEN SILENCE

The morning of Christmas Eve Demi awakens in unfamiliar territory. The sound of a headboard banging against the wall in the room across from her forces her out of her sleep. She looks around and notices shelves of familiar stiletto shoes. She hears the panting of a familiar voice. She thinks to herself,

"How the hell did I end up here?"

She jumps off the queen-sized pillow-top mattress, unfolding herself out of the makeshift bedding.

"Ewww. No sheets. Ain't no telling who used to sleep on this mattress."

She opens the door quietly and walks out into the hallway. She notices all the bedroom doors are closed. She listens closely. She faces the room with the auditory tunes of animal mating seeping from the space underneath the door. She opens it quickly, flinging the door open. Her voice startles the sex mates.

"Well, well, well...look what we have here."

Kennedy turns and faces Demi.

"Twin, you're awake."

Demi stares at Kennedy.

"So you're giving him another go. When ya'll finish, I'm gonna need whoever drove me here to drive me where I really lay my head at night."

Ray jumps up.

"Dylan, it's not what you think."

Demi laughs loudly.

"Oh, you didn't get the memo. My name is Demi. Dylan is no more."

Jazmine overhears the ruckus and runs to join the trio.

"Demi, what's going on? Ewww."

Jazmine notices Kennedy's and Ray's naked bodies. She looks down at Ray's legs, and slowly raises her eyes to his penis.

"You and Ray. I thought you said ya'll broke up."

Kennedy looks at everyone.

"We did. Why, does it matter? She pauses briefly as her mind catches up with the chaotic chatter.

"Don't let me find out, Demi...you used to fuck him and now you're fucking Big Rob too! Ewwww!"

Demi laughs.

"Ray, you wanna explain that one while I find my way home?"

Kennedy continues,

"Who the hell is Dylan?"

Ray looks at all the women with a confused look.

"That's what I would like to know."

Jazmine chimes in.

"Let me do the honors...My homegirl, Dylan, has a multiple personality disorder. Right now...she's Demi."

Ray looks dumbfounded.

"Wait. She what?"

He stares at her as if he found out she's an extraterrestrial alien. Then he asks,

"Is it permanent?"

Demi chimes in before Jazmine.

"If I have anything to do with it. Now, for the last time… whoever the fuck brought me here, I'm ready to go."

Demi walks out of the room to go retrieve her belongings from the other room. Ray starts to follow her, but Jazmine grabs his hand to halt his haste.

"Listen, she's in there…she's just hiding from something traumatic. I'm guessing you know what traumatic things I'm talking about."

Ray pauses.

"Wait. It makes sense."

He snatches his hand from Jazmine and follows Demi into the other bedroom. Demi notices his third leg enter the room before she notices his face.

"Kinky boy, you're coming for dessert."

Ray looks into her eyes with confusion.

"Dylan, I know you're in there. Dylan, listen. I just want to say I'm sorry."

Demi smirks.

"Dylan ain't in here, boy…you're such a wimp, running in here. I don't want you, and Dylan sure as hell doesn't either. Go on back in there with your bitch."

Jazmine stands quietly, trying to hear the conversation from the other room as Kennedy pulls on a pair of sweat pants. She sits on the bed and looks back at Jazmine.

"So how long were they together?"

Jazmine walks to the bed and sits on the edge facing Kennedy.

"Not long. A few months."

Kennedy sighs.

"That bastard never told me he was dating anyone. He comes by once in a while. Gives me a release, and I do the same for him."

She gives Jazmine a vulnerable look, then her face hardens.

"So these multiple personalities...Demi and Dylan. How does it work? Who's the real person?"

Jazmine explains with caution.

"Dylan is the real person. As you can see though, right now, Demi is in control. Dylan comes in and out...but for the past week Demi's been constant."

Kennedy vindictively rejoices.

"Sweet. Ain't never turned my face up at a little drama."

Jazmine tries to convince Kennedy of her loyalty.

"Dylan's my best friend, my allegiance is to her, but Demi is a hella fun."

Both women laugh.

Demi appears in the doorway.

"What the hell is so funny? Never mind. Jazmine, let's go."

Kennedy follows the pair to the front door.

"Well, you slept in your new room for the first time. How do you feel?"

Demi pauses with disgust.

"How the hell did I get here? What the fuck? I don't remember nothing...except snorting something real bad. This situation is not looking so grand. There are too many people making decisions, leaving me without control. I'm outta here. Merry Christmas."

Jazmine and Demi walk out the door. Ray stands in the bedroom door still naked. Demi shakes her head as she exits the apartment.

"Flower child...how the hell did we end up here?"

Jazmine looks at Demi as they walk out of the building.

"Girl, you were so buzzed...I was buzzed. The only one who could drive was Kennedy. She took my keys from me and drove my car. So this is where we ended up."

Demi frowns at Jazmine.

"Next time, stay sober."

A sprinkle of white fluff empties onto the highway at a fast pace as Jazmine drives cautiously, trying to avoid sliding and getting stuck in the growing mountains of snow.

Demi is hypnotized by the snowfall.

"This is why I want a SUV. Hope the chief comes through... Speaking of the chief...he asked if the band could play at the anniversary party for him and the wicked witch of the south."

Jazmine screeches with excitement.

"Aww shucks. Hell yeah, I'm down. What day is that?"

Demi responds,

"It's New Year's Eve. They want to bring in the New Year and celebrate their anniversary at the same time."

Jazmine giggles...

"This is ironic. He didn't want to let Dylan play at Club Red on New Year's Eve. Now he wants the band to play for their anniversary."

The girls laugh like villains.

Jazmine pulls up into the Joneses' driveway. She spots Janay's white Land Rover.

"Be on alert. The Grinch is here."

Demi smirks.

"She don't want no mess from me today, plus she doesn't have her badge to throw around."

As Demi steps out of the car, Jazmine beeps the horn and says,

"All right, I'm out. Gotta go and be nice to new stepfather number four. Maybe I can get a truck out of him too!"

Demi walks into Christmas land as the mistletoe rubs the top of her hat when she enters the door. The ringing of bells and bleeding sounds of Christmas carols playing on the radio stumps Demi's pace. Carmen is drinking eggnog, wrapping up last-minute gifts, and baking cookies in the oven. Demi walks in, looks at Carmen with a raised brow, trying to read the mood. Carmen's love for Christmas erases the animosity.

"Well look who's come home...finally. You're just in time for cookies."

Carmen walks past Demi in a pair of red crushed velvet sweatpants and an oversized "Bowl America" T-shirt. Her green-and-white "Kiss me—I'm a Naughty Elf" apron is draped over her neck with the strings dangling at her waist. She hums while walking past Demi to place another wrapped gift under the Christmas tree. She goes into the kitchen and opens the oven to check on the last batch of cookies. She glances over at Demi.

"Your dad...I mean the chief, and Janay will be back soon. They're at the station. He's taken her off suspension."

Demi mumbles sarcastically,

"Good for them."

Carmen looks into the oven.

"What did you say, dear?"

Demi rolls her eyes. Carmen continues,

"The chief says you're going to play at our anniversary party. Does the band take requests?"

Demi smirks as she softens her thoughts.

"Sure. What do you have in mind?"

Later that evening the two slowly bond over chocolate chip cookies and Christmas music. Jonathan and Janay walk through the front door laughing hysterically. They join Carmen and Demi in front of the tree. Carmen is pleased to see her husband and daughter getting along.

"So all is well in father-and-daughter land?"

Jonathan looks at his wife with satisfaction.

"Yes, dear...all is well. Right, Janay?"

Janay responds with a childlike tone, saying,

"Yes, Dad. We've called a truce. Ma, sorry for my behavior."

Carmen looks at Janay.

"Well, are you going to apologize to your sister?"

Janay sarcastically responds,

"Perhaps."

Jonathan interrupts.

"Tonight will be peaceful. Am I clear?"

Everyone submits to his authoritative voice, and agrees in unison.

Jonathan walks out of the living room into the kitchen and opens the refrigerator. He grabs an ice-cold Heineken, pops open the top, and guzzles the fizz down to relieve the stress.

To lighten the intense mood, Carmen races over to the tree to light it. She grabs Jonathan's hand and whispers to him.

"Maybe this will be a new beginning."

Unaware of Dylan's recent transition to Demi, Janay peers at her and rolls her eyes. Demi smiles and walks in between Carmen and Jonathan. Carmen's excitement increases as she begins a new Christmas caroling session. Demi smiles and sings along, igniting a hidden spark of hatred in Janay.

Janay smiles and hums along to her devious thoughts. She pulls out her camera and snaps a picture of her mother, father, and sister. Demi flinches and holds her head. A sharp pain rushes through her temple and the back of her spine. She fights the pain, stands erect, and continues singing—suspicious of Janay.

The family of four spends the rest of the night walking down memory lane of past Christmases. After the midnight hour, Demi remains awake as the rest of the family turns in for the night. Janay retreats to her childhood bedroom where she lies on her bed looking through the recent photos she's captured. She scans the images with pride. Stopping to stare at her greatest piece...she zooms in on Demi onstage in a chambermaid costume, on her knees with a man standing behind her pumping air between her ass and his crotch. She zooms in closer and stares at Demi snorting white powder off the same man's thumb. Janay smiles with vengeance.

Downstairs in the Joneses' living room, Demi sits in front of the fireplace listening to the crackle of the wood and glaring at the Christmas tree. The flashing lights force Demi into a hypnotic state, bringing the onset of a massive headache. Her eyes roll to the back of her head as she sees random stars shooting through the corner of her eyes. She leans her head back against the couch and slips into a deep slumber.

The next morning, Christmas seeps through the whole household. Jonathan eagerly shakes Demi awake.

"Hey, sleepyhead. Wake up. It's Christmas morning. Why didn't you go upstairs to sleep?"

Demi is silent. Jonathan taps Demi again.

"It's time to open gifts."

He grabs her hand and walks her to the window. He opens the blinds and positions her to face the driveway. A bright red ribbon drapes over the front, back, and sides of the white 2011 GMC Yukon. The shiny SUV blends into the white blanket of snow covering the streets, grass, and driveway.

"Merry Christmas, kid...I hope you and Dylan enjoy it."

He looks at Demi and she is silent and confused.

"What's wrong?

Her eyes lighten, and her lashes flash quickly. Dylan has regained control of her body and mind.

"Daddy...my head hurts."

Jonathan looks into her eyes intensely.

"Baby girl. You're back, you're back."

Dylan looks around in confusion.

"What has happened?"

She pauses as she focuses on the ambiance.

"The tree is beautiful. What...I mean, who...I mean, how long have I been asleep?"

Jonathan holds Dylan's hand.

"Sweetheart, you haven't been asleep. Demi was awake. She's had a hold of the reigns...the longest ever."

Dylan looks out the window and looks at Jonathan again.

"Daddy, you didn't."

She excitedly kisses Jonathan on the cheek.

"But I thought..."

She sits on the couch and continues to hold her head, trying to collect her thoughts.

"I've been such a disappointment."

Jonathan chuckles.

"Hard knocks of life. It's normal. My love is unconditional... and I keep my promises...all I want is for you to keep yours."

Dylan stares at her dad, trying to recall the last time they talked. Her heart begins to race. Her mind flashes images of the texts from Big Rob. She has the desire to come clean to avoid disappointing her dad.

"Daddy, I have a confession."

Just as Dylan fixes her mouth to confess the previous incidents that transpired before she transitioned, her mind shifted to focus on the creaking sounds on the stairs. Carmen's cloud of smoke beats her to the doorway. Then the dry hacking cough follows. She stands in the archway of the living room with her new blond Christmas wig. The curly ringlets flow flawlessly, outlining her oval face.

"Good Morning, Joneses...Merry Christmas."

Jonathan and Dylan smile through their annoyance of disruption. Jonathan stands to greet his wife.

"Good morning, dear. Is this a new hat…a gift to yourself?"

Carmen laughs and taps his hand.

"Oh, Jonathan, my wigs are not hats."

She sits on the sofa beside Dylan.

"Good morning, Ms. Demi. Is this where you slept? My nice plush sofa is becoming a comfortable routine for you…huh?"

Dylan is quiet. Carmen looks at her closely, and then looks at Jonathan. She smiles with tears of joy.

"She's back. My baby's back?"

Jonathan grins with pride.

"Yes, dear. She has a bad headache. I guess she fought her way back. Perhaps you were right. Dylan really loves Christmas."

Chapter 16

THE BALL DROPS...FORTY YEARS AND COUNTING

The eve of the upcoming New Year follows a week of enjoyment and happiness, as a calm seeps through Dylan's pores. Her aura exudes a new sense of control and confidence. She pulls in front of Jazmine's house and beeps the horn. While waiting for Jazmine, she glances at her rearview mirror, puckers her lips, and paints on a thin coat of baby pink lip gloss across her lips to highlight the pink matted lipstick. She glances forward at the blue OnStar button. She presses it,

"Call...two-zero-two eight-nine-three three-three-two-two."

The OnStar system repeats the number.

A ringing phone echoes through the Yukon. A voice-mail greeting startles Dylan.

You have reached the voice-mail of Dr. Lynette Roberts. I am out of town and have limited access to my messages. Please leave your name and number, and I will respond to you as soon as I return. If you need immediate assistance, please call, two-zero-two nine-zero-one three-zero-zero-zero. If this is an emergency, please hang up and dial nine-one-one.

A beep chimes as Jazmine opens the passenger door to the Yukon. Dylan speaks excitedly and loudly.

"Hey, Dr. Roberts, this is Dylan Jones. I…uh wanted to call to let you know what's been going on. I'm OK, I guess, but I've lost my prescription. Actually it isn't lost. I found the empty bottle in my closet after finding out my alter has been prowling for a few days. I'm feeling OK. Taking control…I guess. I'm supposed to be taking a test to join the police academy. Who knows. I think…never mind. What I really wanted to say is…well, what should I do about my medicine? The pharmacy won't fill it…not until thirty days since the last fill. So, I guess…well, I guess I'll be talking to you later."

Dylan presses the blue OnStar button to end the call. She looks nonchalantly at Jazmine. She smiles as she rechecks her makeup. Jazmine looks at Dylan with concern.

"So whatcha goin' do about your meds? I mean, what if Demi takes control?"

Dylan smiles briefly, and she shrugs her shoulders.

"Not concerned about it really. I feel good. Gotta ride it out until I can see Dr. Roberts. Besides, life seems good and on the right path for a change."

Jazmine stares at Dylan for a while.

"So you're serious about the police academy? How you goin' do that, work at Club Red, and be the sleazy ho Big Rob wants you to be?"

"I'm gonna tell my dad everything that happened and all of Big Rob's threats. Just waiting on the right time. Then I'll really be free, and I can help bring down Big Rob."

Jazmine looks at Dylan, unconvinced of her newfound outlook.

"What about keeping your dad safe from Big Rob's wrath?"

Dylan stares at the passing cars while they sit at a traffic light. Her heart begins racing at the thought of losing her father. She shrugs her shoulders again.

"My dad can handle him. I don't think his life is in more danger than it is as the chief of police."

In support of Dylan's position, Jazmine tries smiling with ease.

"Is that right? I'm just gonna say it one more time—the freak in you came out that week Demi was in control. Your bad-girl image was worse than before. Almost seemed too natural. I'm not convinced you'll be able to suppress it and Demi, let alone become a good police cadet."

Both girls laugh out loud as they individually visualize two different versions of Dylan stripping as a police cadet while fighting crime, and then stripping while sexing the enemy and his brother while committing crimes as a police cadet.

Dylan slides her favorite Beyoncé CD into the player and chooses her favorite track..."We Like to Party." Both girls sing the lyrics as the bass and treble flow out of the surround system as they head to Dylan's house to prepare for her parents' anniversary party.

Later that night, the brisk fresh winter air steals the breath of all the eager guests entering the foyer of the Franklin Crosswind Mansion. Each guest follows instructions written in the gold foil lettering outlining details of the mandatory all-white attire. The grand ballroom is filled with old, young, nosey, genuine, and hungry guests. Those who can handle the hard liquor line up continuously at the various bars, requesting top-shelf brands, while the modest drinkers yield to red and white wines or lightly stirred cocktails.

The Flaming Rejects stand center stage, demonstrating control and professionalism as they play mild and demographically targeted tunes for all to enjoy. Dylan sings with pride in her winter-white leather miniskirt, white sequined tank top, and white leather stiletto peep-toe ankle boots. Her round hips sway side to side as she bellows out rehearsed tunes of "Can't Be without You," by Mary J. Blige. The guests applaud her as her melodic notes buzz through their ears.

The party planner, Kent Williams, sashays onstage dressed in a white fitted jacket with a black bow tie. His skinny-leg tailored pants fall slightly above his white snake-skin pointed boot. The two-inch squared heel projects him to appear slightly taller than Dylan. He smiles at Dylan as he commandeers the microphone from her. He shoos her off stage and taps the microphone.

"Excuse me. Yoooohooo. Attention, please.

He clears his throat.

"Thank you everyone for celebrating this milestone with the Joneses. Put your hands together and welcome our guests of honor to the stage. Mr. and Mrs. Jones, please make your way."

The crowd's excitement grows as the couple make their way through an opening the crowd makes for them. Carmen is dressed from head to toe in black. The shimmery sequined wedding dress elongates her back and tightly tucks in her mature sixty-year-old hips. Her black wig is pulled high into a carefully pinned and oiled bun, tightly tucked and swirled into a circular art form. Her red lipstick highlights her happiness, as her lips kiss her teeth periodically, leaving a subtle signature of contentment on her front two teeth. Her ears are draped with black teardrop diamonds and her neck is laced with a matching necklace. Jonathan is dressed in an all-black tuxedo, with a black dress shirt, a black glittery cummerbund and black patent leather shoes. His moustache and beard are sharply landscaped, and the only hint of the mandatory all-white attire lies in his monochromatic beard. Jonathan helps his wife onto the stage. Kent Williams hands Jonathan the microphone and walks to the side of the stage. Jonathan faces the crowd and begins speaking passionately.

"Thank you so much for celebrating this occasion with us. Forty years is a gift."

Carmen motions the planner to hand her a microphone. Jonathan continues,

"I spent my youth chasing this woman, and once I caught up to her, I vowed to spend my life loving her.

Carmen chimes in.

"Indeed he did. I put up a fight. Let him think he had me while I was bojangling with others...But when I gave in, life was beautiful."

The crowd laughs and listens intensely to the couple. Jonathan finishes his speech, saying,

"Carmen, I thank you for forty years of love and fidelity."

Carmen smiles and wipes the tears from her eyes.

"I thank you, Jonathan, for loving me, and I vow to give you forty more years of a romantic revolution."

The couple smile and laugh at the inside joke.

Carmen speaks candidly while outlining her shape in the black wedding dress.

"I first would like to thank everyone for adhering to the mandatory all-white attire. I couldn't have pulled it off."

She points to Dylan.

"That's what I used to look like in white. But now the only white I wear is my underwear."

She laughs at herself hysterically. Dylan smiles with pride at her Coca-Cola-bottle-shaped figure. Janay is in the back of the room laughing and sneering remarks through the chuckles.

"Whore!"

Jonathan overpowers the non-comedic routine.

"We have a treat for you, everyone. Take a trip down memory lane with us."

The lights in the ballroom are dimmed, and a large screen glides down from the ceiling on the side of the room. A slideshow presentation rolls from the projector, flashing images of Carmen and Jonathan through the years. The audience laughs, sighs, and laughs again and again at the couple's photos from their early twenties, throughout their ages—thirties, forties, and fifties. Dylan stands off to the side, observing the photos. She realizes she's never seen some of the photos. She notices an image of a thuggish-looking man in a couple of the photos with her father. Simultaneously she catches a glimpse of her mother walking through the crowd, headed to the exit of the ballroom. Carmen is talking to an older version of the man that stood in the background of some of the images with her father and mother. She walks toward the exit, but Janay forcefully snatches her by the arm, pulling her into a dark corner in the hallway. Janay appears drunk and is wearing an unflattering white dress with round-toe white pumps. Dylan looks at her defensively.

"Get your fucking hands off me."

Janay laughs out loud.

"What—are you taking a stand against me?"

Dylan slyly responds,

"I've avoided you all night and plan on keeping it that way."

Janay stares at her with malice in her eyes. Dylan smiles connivingly and manages to slip in a defense strategy to break away from Janay.

"Let me guess; you're mad because Mommy gave me and my figure a shout-out?"

Janay rolls her eyes and stares blankly at Dylan as she straightens the pleats in her dress. She opens her black hobo, pulls out a brown envelope, and hands it to her sister. Dylan cautiously opens the envelope and sifts through the contents. She pulls out a stack of photos.

Janay laughs.

"I gotta hand it to myself. I did a great job. Too bad I didn't get a chance to add them to Dad's slideshow. Can you imagine the look on all of their faces?" She laughs loudly.

Dylan sifts through the images with confusion and unfamiliarity. She smiles and laughs indulgently.

"You graduated first in your class, huh? You fucking twit. You're so focused on my life you didn't look at the fine details. This isn't me...I mean it's my body, but certainly not my mind. Look at my expression. This is Demi all the way."

Dylan laughs and slides out of the hostile corner.

Dylan walks back into the ballroom, and her father is talking to a handsome man of average height, athletically built. He's in an all-white tuxedo. His razor-sharp goatee accentuates his cocoa complexion. His soft waves mesmerize the many women walking past. Jonathan spots Dylan, and he reaches out for her hand to slow her angered pace. He smiles proudly.

"Dylan...Dylan...sweetheart. Slow down. I want to introduce you to someone."

Dylan smiles bashfully as his white smile and straight teeth magnetically draw her in. The masculine scent of musk, vanilla, and juniper entices her with every breath she takes in to fill her lungs. Jonathan formally introduces the two.

"Kenneth Smith, this is my princess, Dylan. She's the one I've promised to you."

Dylan swings her head to stare at her father.

"Wait...what? Promised. What is this? We don't live in ancient times."

Kenneth smiles, and speaks with a mesmerizing tone.

"Don't take it that way. I've been inquiring about you for months. Your beauty and your smile hypnotized me in the photos on his desk. I just wanted to meet you."

Dylan smiles calmly.

"So this wasn't his idea? OK. At least you have your own agenda. He just doesn't get that my dating choices are mine."

Satisfied with his daughter's submission and Kenneth's charm, Jonathan excuses himself after spotting the party planner walking onstage. Jonathan looks at his watch and realizes that the stroke of midnight is fast approaching. Jonathan walks onstage and takes the microphone to alert the guests to grab their loved ones to prepare for the countdown to the New Year. Dylan makes her way back onto the stage to join the band as they play one more set before the ball drops. Jonathan walks out into the hall searching for his wife with ten minutes to spare.

Carmen is in a side room talking to an unexpected and uninvited guest. She's smiling and grinning ear to ear, laughing at his welcomed yet inappropriate jokes.

Farther down the hall, Janay exits the women's bathroom with her head down as she mumbles undeserving rants about Dylan. She fumbles through her black hobo purse looking for her flask. She decides to walk outside to enjoy her drink away from the celebration. As she exits the mansion, she runs smack into Big Rob. She excuses herself, not realizing who he is. Big Rob stares at her with a smirk on his face. Janay looks him directly in his eyes as they pierce through her soul. She stares blankly as chills climb the back of her spine. She tilts her flask, and all the vodka inside pours out, as he leans into her and sucks her face with his tongue and lips. Janay recovers from the brief shock, wipes her face, and then pushes him playfully.

"It was you…it was you. You're here, not locked down or dead."

Big Rob leans into her again and kisses her neck.

Janay continues,

"What the fuck...I can't believe it."

Big Rob smiles.

"It's me. Look at you. All fresh in your white."

Janay smiles ear to ear,

"Oh my god. My heart is racing like it used to in the stairway at school."

Janay leans into Big Rob and kisses him.

Inside the ballroom, Dylan is onstage rocking out to her song on the drums. Jazmine is singing behind the beat of one of Prince the Artist's classic songs, "1999," remixing her own lyrics.

"*Two thousand eleven and we're almost out of time, tonight we're partying hard 'cause it's almost twenty twelve.*"

Dylan rocks the drums and loses the beat as she catches a glimpse of Ray in the dancing crowd. She struggles to gather her focus and then loses his silhouette in the cloud of blazing lights and holiday shimmer.

With only two minutes to spare, Jonathan catches the sound of Carmen's laugh down the crowded hall as everyone is rushing to the ballroom in time to join in for the countdown. Carmen looks at her watch and starts to walk away from her uninvited guest, but he instantly grabs her arm, pulls off his white cap, and holds her against the wall. He looks into her eyes and caresses her face, while leaning into to her attractive red lips. Carmen slides her hands inside his white pinstriped sports coat and rubs his waist and back. She slides her hands down his winter-white wool pants. The crowd inside the ballroom chants loudly, counting down to the last five seconds before the stroke of midnight. The last number of the countdown is bellowed out through the walls.

Just as the uninvited guest brushes Carmen's face with his, Jonathan walks up. He shouts abruptly,

"Russell Kendrick...get your filthy hands off my wife."

He looks at Carmen with disgust and contempt. Russell Kendrick turns to face Jonathan. He smiles, while wiping Carmen's red lipstick off his lips with the back of his hand.

"Jonathan Jones...I'm sorry. Chief Jones. Just thought I'd drop in and congratulate the couple. Couldn't find you, so I thought I'd reminisce on old times with my...I mean, what used to be mine."

Jonathan forcefully grabs Russell by the forearm.

"No uninvited guests are welcome here."

Russell scuffles out of Jonathan's grip.

"I'll catch you two later. By the way...nice slideshow. Thanks for including me in the tribute."

Russell chuckles as he exits the mansion. He spots Big Rob on the side of the building kissing Janay. He walks over to the two hormonal kissing birds.

"Young blood...let's go...now!"

Janay notices Russell and has flashes of her teenage memories. She smiles with excitement.

"Hi, Mr. Kendrick."

Russell winks at her and hops into his gold 2008 Cadillac. Big Rob lets go of Janay's hand and follows his father's lead. Janay shouts,

"Wait...don't leave me again. You can't."

Big Rob looks empathetically at her and looks at his father. She can see the two of them talking back and forth. Russell looks at his son and says,

"She might be useful."

Big Rob steps out of the passenger door and opens the back right passenger door. Janay hesitates and then runs toward the Cadillac. Just as she climbs in the back, Ray runs out the front door of the mansion and hops in the back with her. Carmen and Jonathan make their way to the front entrance as they observe the gold Cadillac pulling off with their daughter in the back. He looks at Carmen with disgust and sarcastically speaks before walking away.

"I guess this is the beginning of a new revolution."

Chapter 17

REUNITED AND IT FEELS...

SO DIFFERENT

Exactly twelve hours after the celebratory event, the New Year isn't so exciting. The happily married couple of forty years aren't so happy. Jonathan stands in his robe drinking a beer, glaring out the window. With each swig of beer, he sweats harder and struggles through each flashing memory of the night before. The one person he despised touched the one person he loved and trusted; she got too close with the enemy. Carmen appears in front of her husband half-dressed from the night before. Her lips are stained from the red lipstick. She pleads for his sympathy.

"Jonathan...talk to me.

Jonathan opens another beer and proceeds to guzzle it down.

Carmen continues,

"Jonathan, you have to talk to me. It was not my fault. He... well, you know he has a weird effect on me."

Jonathan slams the beer on the table and punches the wall.

"Did you invite him?

Carmen pauses with confusion.

"No. I saw him walking through the crowd."

Jonathan continues with his interrogation.

"Well how the hell did he know about our party?"

Carmen stares blankly in search of the answer. She whispers with caution as she hears movement on the top level.

"I don't know. Perhaps someone back home showed him the invitation."

Jonathan scratches his head.

"No one from Jamaica was there."

"I know, but I sent an announcement."

Jonathan grunts with disgust.

"Unbelievable. After forty years, and this is how you show your love for me. Swapping spit with your ex-lover."

Carmen nervously explains,

"It was innocent. You have the real deal. Look at it like I was giving him closure."

Jonathan sits down and stares at his wife. Dylan overhears the couple as she creeps downstairs. She catches the tail end of the couple's discussion. She asks with concern,

"What's wrong, Daddy?"

The couple look at Dylan and halt their intense debate. Jonathan looks at his daughter and smiles.

"Nothing, baby girl. Just a misunderstanding."

Dylan grabs some cereal and heads back upstairs to her room where she left Jazmine snoring. She keeps her door cracked, so she can listen in on what they're arguing about. Carmen sits down beside Jonathan and places his hand in her hand.

"You know I love you, honey…there is no other man for me."

Jonathan looks at Carmen's distress and kisses her ring finger. He grins.

"I sure hope it's true…'cause shit is going to hit the fan. Russell's probably already brainwashing Janay. After all these years, I'd thought she'd forgotten about that delinquent of a son...Mr. Robert Kendrick."

Carmen walks over to the stove to fix Jonathan a plate of grilled salmon, cornbread, and spinach. She places his plate in front of him and sighs.

"So what do we do?"

Jonathan leans over his plate to pray. He looks up at his wife,

"First things first...I'm putting surveillance on him and his crew. Gotta find out what he's in town for. Then I'm keeping Dylan close. I've already got a team ready to keep close watch on her. I will be damned if he gets his hands on my baby girl."

Dylan listens from her cracked-open bedroom door. She closes the door slowly to avoid her parents' discovery of her eavesdropping. She stands over Jazmine's snoring body.

"Jazmine...wake up."

Jazmine wakes up from her deep sleep with crust in the corner of her eyes and an ashy trace of dried spit in the corners of her mouth. She tightly grips the covers over her head to ward off Dylan's insistent demand for morning gossip. Dylan's consistent attempt to wake her forces her to release her tight grip on the comforter, while Dylan drags her out of the bed. Both girls stand in the walk-in closet as Dylan paces back and forth anxiously. Jazmine sits on the stool inside the closet and awaits Dylan's frantic news.

Dylan says nervously,

"My father knows Big Rob and his father."

Jazmine waits to register the information, and then responds,

"How do you know?"

Dylan nervously responds,

"I overheard him talking to my mother. Apparently my mother used to date Big Rob's father."

Jazmine gasps.

"This shit just got weirder. So not only have you fucked both brothers, your mother has fucked their father."

Dylan sighs.

"I don't know. I think my father and Big Rob's father used to be friends. My dad caught the father kissing on my mother."

Jazmine gasps with shock and holds her hand over her mouth.

"Noooo. Not at the party. Was that what all that commotion outside the party was about?"

Dylan nods her head and shrugs her shoulders in disbelief.

"I think so."

She sighs.

"And I think Janay is hooked in this mess some kind of way too. My dad mentioned Big Rob's father brainwashing Janay and that he's got a security detail scheduled to follow me everywhere. He said he's going to prevent him from getting his hands on me."

Jazmine looks bewildered.

"Whose hands...Big Rob?"

Dylan sucks her teeth in frustration.

"No dummy...the father."

Jazmine pauses briefly, then has an epiphany.

"Oh. I was about to say...both sons already got a hold of that ass."

Both girls giggle momentarily. Then Dylan regains seriousness.

"This isn't funny, Jaz...now I really can't tell my dad about all the incidents."

Across town in the Kendricks' lair, Janay snuggles peacefully under Big Rob's broad arms. As she awakes, she decides to surprise him with a rekindled gesture. She slides down to his waist and wakes him with a slow stride of suckling noises, encasing his nutsack between the folds of her jaws. Big Rob begins to groan out of his slumber and mumbles words of satisfaction. He gets louder.

"Ooohhhh, Dylan...damn, girl."

Janay stops and unleashes his hairy balls. Big Rob continues,

"Ooohhh...don't stop."

Janay sits up, punches him in the chest.

"I know you didn't just call me Dylan. Are you fucking kidding me? Now you got that bitch's name on the brain. I bet it was that skanky-ass white leather skirt."

Big Rob opens his eyes and realizes Janay is sitting in front of him spewing fire.

"Oh...Janay. My bad. Just a crazy dream."

Janay jumps up and starts dressing herself in her all-white attire.

"What the fuck is this? You drop off the face of the earth for twenty years and show up at my parents' anniversary party. And then you have fire in your pants for my sister. How do you even know her name?"

Before Big Rob can respond, Ray walks into Big Rob's room without knocking.

"'Ey, Rob...Dad wants you. It seems you gotta a lot of explaining to do. Oh yeah...he said bring the cop too."

Big Rob picks up a shoe and throws it at the bedroom door. Ray runs out the room laughing.

Big Rob jumps up and puts on a pair of heather-gray sweat pants and a T-shirt. He looks at Janay and smiles.

"When father summons we all follow. Hurry and come down when you are decent."

Janay joins the Kendrick trio in the sunroom on the side of the drafty house. She looks around at the expensive furniture and appliances. She hears the sons talking to the father about sports. As soon as she enters the room, Russell Kendrick turns and smiles at Janay.

"Good morning, beautiful. How did you sleep?"

Janay stands coldly and answers with an annoyed tone.

"Fine."

Russell grins and shuffles around in his house slippers. He turns down the flat-screen television in the kitchen, and he points to a chair for Janay to sit.

"It's been a long time."

Janay speaks through her smile, saying,

"I agree."

Russell continues,

"I see your love continues to burn for my son."

Janay frowns and says,

"I thought it did."

Russell rubs his round belly and folds his arms.

"Well, do you remember your father tried to put that fire out back when ya'll were teenagers?"

Janay rolls her eyes as she reminisces,

"I remember. I was brokenhearted."

Big Rob starts pacing around his father and Janay.

He appears anxious as Russell continues to visit the past with Janay.

Russell continues,

"Well, he did some other stuff too—ruined my son's life."

Janay rudely responds,

"Really. How did he do that?"

Russell laughs with contempt.

"Don't act surprised."

Janay becomes agitated.

"I am...I know my father is protective, but I wouldn't blame his forceful hand for breaking up me and Rob or...or for ruining his life."

Janay's eyes begin to water, and she continues,

"I actually thought your son ran off, got caught up in illegal activities, and ended up in jail or possibly dead. My heart fell to my knees when I saw him last night."

Russell grows bored with her love jams and the silent violins playing in the back of his mind. He quickly realizes she'll probably protect her father. He stands up and snaps his fingers. He rudely shouts to Big Rob,

"Show Sergeant Jones to the door. This isn't going to work out."

Janay stands up and screeches loudly to Big Rob,

"What is this? You like ripping my soul out of me?"

Big Rob appears uneasy and sympathetic to Janay's cries.

He strokes her face and kisses her on the cheek.

"Janay...my father's right. You're a cop. I'm a bad boy. This will never work."

Janay cries hysterically as Big Rob closes the door in her face. A cab pulls up and waits outside the large stone-and-brick house. Janay collects herself and walks off the porch toward the cab. She sits inside, slams the door, and sits silently for a few seconds before realizing the driver was waiting for an address. Tears roll steadily down her face as she struggles to blurt out her address with her trembling voice. She stares out the window and sobs all the way to her house.

Chapter 18

TWENTY-ONE AND OVER

The morning of January 7 greets the sun as the moon disappears over the horizon. The white wooden blinds are slightly open, allowing a hint of the sun to peer through. The sound of a clucking rooster blazes through the alarm clock sitting on Dylan's nightstand. The next sound to ring through the speakers is the sound of the 95.5 FM radio personality screaming, "Wake up!" in an attempt to alert all the sleeping beauties and beasts that the seventh hour is upon them.

Dylan peels her eyes open slowly, rolls over, and slams her hand on the clock to eliminate the noise. Twenty minutes later, the snooze alert sounds off a ringing noise that motivates Dylan to immediately jump out of her comfortable warm sheets. She stands in front of her mirror and glances at the calendar. She leans in and focuses on a circled date on her wall calendar. Dylan smiles at the red circle ornamenting the date, January 7, with happy faces and small hearts. She leans in toward the mirror and whispers to herself,

"Birthday girl…gotta say…you don't look a day over twenty-one."

She kisses the mirror and stretches. The sound of her cell phone receiving text messages startles her as she bonds with herself. Dylan jumps on her bed, starts scrolling through her phone, and reads all the birthday wishes from her band mates, Jazmine, and an unknown number. She leans over the side of her bed and grabs her wallet out of her purse. In search of the fortieth anniversary napkin she saved with the cute lawyer's scribbled number, she rummages through the contents quickly. After a minute looking through her wallet and bag, she finds the paper and reads the written words *Kenneth Smith, 202.455.6212.* She compares the number to the unfamiliar number displayed on her cell phone's screen. She smiles. Kenneth's message entices her.

"*Good morning, beautiful. I hear it's your birthday. Make each minute count.*"

Dylan smiles and responds,

"Is this the person my hand has been promised to? If so... proper courting is mandatory."

As she waits for Kenneth to respond, she walks to her closet to search for the proper birthday outfit. Her eyes lock on three FSW boxes that she's purposely saved for a special occasion. She flips open the top of one of the boxes that houses a pair of deep-royal-blue peep-toe pumps with a black glass bow resting over the open toe area. The smoky glasslike heel elongates the pure masterpiece. Dylan slips the shoe onto her freshly manicured toes from her "girls' day out" with Jazmine the day before. As she ponders over an outfit that would accentuate her footwear, she's interrupted by her ringing landline. Just as she lifts the handset from the base of the phone, she hears her best friend's voice screeching through the phone, backed up by the acoustic rhythm from the electronic keyboard.

"*I hear it's your birthday, and you're grown and sexy—rock it, girl, rock it, girl...*"

Dylan laughs humbly. Jazmine finishes the short birthday song, laughing at her impromptu celebration.

"What's up, D…what's planned for the day? I think drinks and dancing should be the main attraction."

Dylan pauses with consideration.

"I'm down, but we're going to have an entourage of bodyguards. You know my dad is on high alert."

The two girls exchange ideas as to where their first, middle, and last club tours should take place. After the girls discuss potential outfits and shoes, they agree on the kickoff time for the celebration. When Dylan ends her call with Jazmine, her taste buds grow erect on her tongue as her nostrils flare at the scent of buttered biscuits, grits, scrambled eggs, and pancakes, all prepared by her mother's hands. She hastens downstairs to the kitchen and is greeted by a full buffet spread in the dining room. Carmen comes out with a cigarette hanging from her lips, holding a dish of scrambled eggs and cheese, seeping with steam. She mumbles through the small crack between her grayish-brown lips and the stiff cigarette,

"Happy birthday, sweetie."

The sound of growling stomachs fighting for attention grows stronger as Dylan and Jonathan walk in the dining room simultaneously. Jonathan smiles at Dylan with pride and speaks proudly,

"Twenty-one years…someone has reached the threshold. Happy birthday, baby girl."

He kisses her on the cheek and sits down beside her. Dylan smiles. Jonathan looks at Dylan as he grabs the basket of freshly baked biscuits.

"Whatcha got planned today?"

Dylan looks up at her father and reveals small details about the celebratory night she and her sidekick, Jazmine, have planned. She dodges in and out of fine lines of white lies and formalities, strategically maneuvering away from the hidden truths of nonstop heavy drinking and possible one-night stands.

Chief Jones agrees to loosen the reins on her security detail and assigns only two bodyguards to drive her and her friends around in her SUV.

Later on that evening, around 9:00 p.m., Dylan steps out of her closet wearing a pair of rich deep-plum skinny jeans, a fitted white shirt with gold lettering, gold hoop earrings, three multi-length gold necklaces, gold bangles, the royal-blue peep-toe heels and a vintage biker-styled soft gray leather jacket. She paints a deep layer of her favorite MAC Viva Glam II lavender lipstick on her lips and highlights her pucker with a swipe of her favorite purple lip gloss. She mashes her lips together and walks out of her bedroom door on the path to her night of birthday bliss and mayhem.

The two bodyguards wait patiently outside Dylan's white Yukon parked in the driveway of the Joneses' estate. As soon as Dylan hops in, she instructs the driver to pick up her best friend, Jazmine, first and then two of her band mates. As soon as the birthday entourage is joined for the night of fun, their first destination of drinking and dancing begins at Club Nine. Dylan instructs the driver to drop them off at Club Nine. After two hours of nonstop toasts and shots of Patron and lemon drops filled with Grey Goose, the girls convince the bodyguards to take them to Club Red.

As the Yukon turns out of parking lot of Club Nine, the driver spots an all-black Chevy Impala tailing behind, but he is so enthralled in the extreme levels of estrogen bouncing off the roof of the SUV, he forgets to mention his observation to the other bodyguard. All four girls are advanced, past the line of eagerly and equally hormonally induced girls waiting to get inside the club after the bouncer, who has a crush on Jazmine, lets them inside. The bodyguards begin to relax more since the crowd isn't as aggressive as Club Nine, and the bouncers are familiar with Dylan and Jazmine.

One hour after the girls' cocktail appetites are satisfied, all four begin to seductively dance on the dance floor while grinding and gyrating to the beat of the DJ's playlist of recently released hits. Kennedy is walking through the crowd and spots the dancing birthday diva and waves to her. Dylan continues to dance wildly. Jazmine leans into Dylan. She tries to prepare her for the impending interaction.

"Don't look now, but the chick that is walking up to you is Kennedy."

Dylan turns too soon. Kennedy is standing in front of Dylan smiling,

"What's up, twin? You changed your mind? Don't want to be roommates?"

Dylan stares blankly and pauses before speaking,

"Kennedy, right?"

Kennedy remembers the crazy conversation between her and Jazmine at the apartment regarding Dylan's disorder.

"Oh, wait. Let me guess. You're not Demi."

She laughs without compassion.

"Is Demi in there...gotta talk with my homegirl. She's a blast."

Dylan rolls her eyes, and turns to dance away from Kennedy. Jazmine and Kennedy make eye contact. Jazmine walks closer to Kennedy.

"Hey, Kennedy. What's up?

The bass of the music pumps louder and vibrates Jazmine's voice as she tries to engage her thoughts with Kennedy.

"How's it going?"

Kennedy looks coldly at Jazmine.

"Nothing...evidently. No roommate, no man. Nothing."

Kennedy walks away, leaving the dancing tribe to their celebration. An hour later, Kennedy is in the back of the club in the locker room puffing on a blunt filled with marijuana. Big Rob walks in and pulls Kennedy to the side. He whispers to her, filling her seductive mind with an earful of mischief and intrigue. Thirty minutes later, Kennedy is back on the dance floor seeking attention from Jazmine, trying to engage her in conversation.

"Hey, Jazmine, bring Dylan back to the locker room. I want to get to know her...plus there's a lot of party treats in the back—if you know what I mean."

Jazmine winks in agreement and convinces Dylan to go the back room for a treat.

"You said you wanted to drink, party, and rock out to drugs tonight...let's go have some real fun."

Dylan's inebriated mind agrees. She assures the bodyguards that she is going to the bathroom, and they didn't need to follow. Dylan follows Jazmine to the back and is greeted with more cocktails, marijuana pipes, and cocaine. Dylan's arousal seeps outward as she envisions a night full of wasteful bliss for her twenty-first birthday. She sits down on the lounge chair next to Jazmine. Kennedy starts up random conversation.

"So how long you been living with the craziness in your mind?"

Dylan stares blankly at Kennedy, shocked at the bluntness. She responds,

"It's called multiple personalities. What's it to you?"

Kennedy smirks slyly.

"I met the other side of you. She's cool. I'm just curious how it works."

Dylan raises her brow.

"There's no science to it...I don't think."

Kennedy grows irritable.

"So you're the bitch that Ray is hung up on?"

Dylan grows defensive.

"Excuse me?"

As soon as Dylan's tone rises, gunshots ring out outside the lounge door. Jazmine and Dylan jump up, and Kennedy punches Dylan in her face, knocking her out cold. Jazmine rushes toward Dylan and is knocked over the head with a bottle. The sound of screaming partygoers blazes through the air as Big Rob and his crew rush the back lounge. Big Rob is screaming through the pain of his bloody ear. He looks at Kennedy and cues her to follow the plan.

"Tie them bitches up. Where is Ray? He can help."

He looks for a towel to wipe the blood off his face.

"The fuckin' bitch-ass bodyguards tried to buck. Try to stop me from walking in my fuckin' club. Fuck that."

Kennedy, Big Rob, and four members of his crew pile in the black Suburban, with Dylan and Jazmine bound and gagged. As the truck peels out of the back alley, a black Chevy Impala with tints drives eight cars behind them.

The screaming sirens on the scout car of every available police officer sound through the streets, heading to Club Red. Witnesses and bystanders are giving testimony to the events in chronological order in bits and pieces. No one knows the one thing that the police are seeking to find out—who the gunmen are.

The next morning, Dylan wakes up in Kennedy's apartment with her hands bound and her mouth gagged. She's barefoot. She struggles to look through her puffy black eye as tears stream down her face. She feels a burning pulse through the tears of her cracked lip. She mumbles for help.

"Mmmmmm...help."

The cracking sound of her quivering voice wakes Jazmine. She tries to sit up and realizes her hands are tied. She hears Dylan's struggle to call out again.

Jazmine tries to scoot over to Dylan to comfort her and to let her know she's not alone.

Big Rob bursts through the door. He grabs Dylan and stands her up. He unties the gag from behind her head.

"Awwwe, look at you, little princess. Hear you've been busy...hear her name is Demi...I want to see Demi. We got good chemistry."

Dylan rolls her eyes at Big Rob. He continues,

"I fell in love with her...and the only way I'll go easy is if she comes back. I told you to follow my rules from day one. So not only will your daddy die, but you will too!"

He pauses...

"However, I'll make a deal with you...bring Demi back, and I'll let you live."

Dylan fights off the onset of trickling streams of salt-water pellets. Her heart begins to race out of fear of losing control of her lucid state of mind. She closes her eyes and begins praying for the strength to fight her sociopathic brain and hold Demi at bay. In the presence of her psychotic captor, Dylan's fear grows larger with thoughts of a potential traumatic binge creeping onto the horizon. An impending doom scribbles details in her mind, an outline of her permanent life of destruction.

Chapter 19

WHAT HAPPENED IN VEGAS?

The sound of rage and organized chatter resonates outside the doors and windows of the Metropolitan Police Station. Over two hundred uniformed police officers of various ranks stand erect in an oval huddle inside the lobby of the station. Chief Jonathan Jones's distinctive angry voice echoes rants of vindictive rage.

"I want all available bodies knocking down doors of every crooked punk in this city. Use every resource…threaten every source. Do whatever you have to in order to bring back my princess. Our very own lost their lives last night trying to protect her. Find my baby girl now."

As soon as Chief Jones dismisses his staff, everyone disperses, except Sergeant Foster. He follows the chief to his office, and closes the door behind them.

"Chief…I'm at your beck and call. I will spend night and day getting her back, and bring down those responsible."

Chief Jones nods his head with appreciation. Before the two have a chance to discuss details of possible leads, Janay interrupts the conversation.

"Dad, can I talk to you?"

Chief Jones excuses Sergeant Foster to talk privately with Janay. When Sergeant Foster exits the office, Janay sits down in front of her father's desk.

"Dad...you're doing all of this for what? What if Dylan is responsible for all of this? It's her alter ego's motive."

Chief Jones looks at Janay with disgust.

"You're telling me you think Dylan walked into Club Red and shot her bodyguards, innocent bystanders, and some of my plainclothes cops? Really. I gotta hand it to you. This is your all-time low. If you're not here to do your job, then perhaps this isn't where you belong. Besides, some question if you have recently been turned."

Janay stands up and starts cursing at her father.

Chief Jones doesn't bat an eyelash.

"Janay, I don't have time for one of your temper tantrums."

Janay's voice increases with rage and disrespect.

"I can't believe you think I would disrespect my badge."

Chief Jones chuckles.

"It's certainly not the first time. Tell me, what business did you have with the Kendrick clan? I didn't put you on any surveillance detail."

He pulls out an envelope and reveals a stack of pictures. The images captured are photos of her parked in a black Chevy Impala, photos of her taking pictures, kissing Big Rob, sleeping in Big Rob's bed, and snorting cocaine with Big Rob.

He looks at Janay with disappointment. He walks over to his flat-screen television, turns it on, and presses play on the DVD player.

"A good cop always digs deep in an investigation. A bad cop always leaves a trail."

Chief Jones sits down and bashes the heels of his shoes onto his desk. Janay sits and watches images of herself on the television captured from inside Club Red, outside the club, and on the street. She's inside the club snorting cocaine, talking to the bodyguards, leading the bodyguards away from Dylan and her friends, talking in the hallway to Big Rob, hitting Jazmine over the head, running out of the back room, walking outside the club, and getting into the black Chevy Impala.

Janay stares blankly at the screen. She's speechless. Chief Jones shuts the television off. He speaks with a vengeful tone.

"Sgt. Janay Jones, as chief of police of the Metropolitan Police Department, it is my duty to inform you that you've been permanently dismissed from your duties until further notice, upon the completion of the ethics review board. Please hand over your badge and your weapon. Clean your locker out and leave the premises. You will have a chance to appeal the decision after the investigation with the ethics board."

Before he finishes, Janay storms out of his office without leaving her gun. She rushes past Sergeant Foster who is sitting on the edge of Chief Jones's secretary's desk. She mutters threats and rants to Sergeant Foster.

"You piece of scum, you fake-ass wannabe son. He's all yours. He's dead to me."

Sergeant Foster smirks at Janay as she rushes on to the elevator. He winks at her as the doors close.

Sergeant Foster returns to the chief's office.

"Chief Jones…is there anything else you need me to do? I'm going to brief my team, so we can bring Dylan home."

Chief Jones looks up from reading his notes on his desk.

"No that's it for the night."

Chief Jones stands up and walks over to Sergeant Foster.

"Son, I want to thank you for the outstanding surveillance and having the balls to bring it to my attention. Keep up the good work."

Sergeant Foster smiles with pride.

"No thanks needed, sir…it was my pleasure."

Big Rob is pacing back and forth in Kennedy's apartment, looking out the window.

"Where the hell is Ray? Something's is wrong."

Kennedy tries to calm him by bringing Big Rob a plate of food.

"Bitch, I ain't hungry. We gotta get out of here."

Kennedy shuffles through the kitchen with her sexy lingerie and high-heeled slippers. She looks at Big Rob with confusion.

"But what about those two in the room?"

Big Rob looks out the window. He punches the wall and says angrily,

"Oh, the crazy one is coming with us. If only we can turn her, it would be so much easier."

Kennedy sits down as she tries to remember her conversation with Jazmine. She remembers.

"Her sidekick said stress and fear bring Demi out. It's not a guarantee but worth the try."

Big Rob strokes his goatee.

"Well, I guess that's my cue."

Kennedy smiles with excitement at seeing Demi again. She pushes Big Rob to the direction of the bedroom where Dylan and Jazmine are tied up.

"Just hurry up. I don't want the heat busting down the door. I like it here."

Big Rob returns to the room where Dylan and Jazmine are tied up. He waves a white towel.

"I come in peace."

Jazmine wakes up again. He unties the two bruised beauties.

"Listen up. We're going on a little trip."

Jazmine's startled mind brings on survival thoughts. She yells,

"I'm not going anywhere...the second location is where you'll kill us off."

Jazmine starts screaming. Big Rob leans over and punches her in her face, knocking her out cold. Dylan stares into space, showing no emotion. She's concentrating hard, fighting off a loss of control, but she soon realizes in order to survive Big Rob she must play his game. She looks at Big Rob and tries to remember what Jazmine described as Demi behavior.

"Hey, gorgeous. Long time no see. How about reuniting those lips with mine."

Big Rob stands up and walks back over to Dylan. He looks deep into her eyes.

"Demi…is that really you?"

Dylan exudes a conniving smile.

"I'm glad you put her screaming ass to sleep. How about some one-on-one time bonding with my pussycat and your snake."

Big Rob pauses and buys into her Demi act.

"You're back. This snake has missed swirling in that grass. Let's get you cleaned up first. We're taking a trip."

Dylan breathes slowly to concentrate on her role. She allows Big Rob to undress her and walk her into the bathroom. He steps into the shower with her and lets the warm stream from the showerhead wash the bruised blood away from her eyes and lips. Dylan closes her eyes and summons the ways of Demi. She feels Big Rob kissing all over her body. He's widened her legs and starts munching his way into a frenzy, leaving her legs buckling at the onset of a thirty-second pulsating climax. He turns her over, facing her toes, as he enters her forest from behind. The rhythmic strokes send her into a trance, setting off a ringing in her head with a pinch of a headache. She screams through his release.

ⅇ⤳

Three hours later, she awakens in a plush seat on a private plane. She hears the cackling laughter of Kennedy talking on her cellphone. She catches the last few words of Big Rob's conversation to someone on the phone.

"I haven't heard from baby brother in two days. I think something bad has happened to him."

Dylan's eyes begin to tear up at the thought of another person dying in the midst of the chaos. She leans forward in search of Jazmine. Big Rob continues talking.

"Clean up the mess at Kennedy's spot. It's small. Won't give too much fight. Just make the dump somewhere isolated."

Dylan decodes Big Rob's subtle hints and realizes that he's talking about Jazmine. She stands up and heads to the back of the plane in search for the restroom. Kennedy is suspicious of Big Rob's success in forcing Demi to the forefront of Dylan's mind, so she follows Dylan to the back of the plane.

"What are you looking for, a phone to call for help?"

Dylan stops and turns quickly, ensuring she doesn't miss a beat.

"Twin…whatcha talking about? I'm just looking for the bathroom."

She looks down at her sparkling pants and stripper pumps.

"Thanks for the outfit. We are definitely twins now."

Dylan enters the bathroom and takes a look at her gold sparkling skinny stretch pants with a red halter top and a white tank top spilling from underneath. She notices the pound of concealer and foundation that has hidden her black eye and swollen lips. Dylan laughs at her new look.

"She's created a clone. I'm officially a stripper gone rogue."

Dylan returns to her seat beside Big Rob. She inquires about Jazmine.

"Is Jazmine coming with us?"

Big Rob and Kennedy look at Dylan and pause.

"I'm just asking...she is normally stuck up my ass, so not having her around feels different."

She pauses.

"Anyway...where are we going?"

Big Rob looks over at Dylan and grins.

"The one place where no one will ever search for us."

Dylan stares blankly. Kennedy blurts out,

"Vegas, bitch. Where sins don't have to be forgiven."

The trio checks into a top-floor suite at the Wynn Resort & Casino. Big Rob gets excited, as he has a lot of work to do for his plan to be executed well. He leaves Kennedy and Dylan in the suite and goes out to meet with his crew of thugs who have flown down to meet him.

Back at casa Kennedy, Ray walks into the condo in search of his brother and ex-girlfriend. His frantic search reveals a bruised and dehydrated Jazmine. He wakes her up and puts two packs of frozen vegetables on her face and the back of her head. Ray gently wipes away the bruised blood from her face and her wrists. He tries to get her to talk.

"Jazmine...talk to me. What happened?"

Jazmine ignores him. He continues to nurse her bruises. Ray goes into the kitchen and makes some soup and toast to help ignite some energy into Jazmine. An hour later— and after three bowls of chicken noodle soup with toast and Oreo Cookies—Jazmine starts regaining strength. She's ready to talk. She looks up at Ray and shakes her head. She starts searching for her security fingerless gloves to cover her wrists. Ray looks at her as she frantically tries to cover her scars.

"Did you do that to your wrists?"

Jazmine looks away from Ray. She pulls the gloves over her wrists.

Ray continues,

"Jazmine, please help me understand...did you do this to yourself, or did they do this to you?"

Jazmine starts crying quietly to herself. The tears stream like a broken faucet.

Ray walks over to her and hugs her.

"Why do you hurt yourself?"

Jazmine pauses and cries through her explanation.

"I don't mean to...it just helps me forget about the pain."

She cries uncontrollably.

"No one ever noticed...or ever asked. Not even Dylan."

Ray continues to hug her.

"I noticed, and I care. Please don't hurt yourself."

Jazmine looks up at Ray and extends her plump lips toward his. Ray kisses Jazmine and caresses her. Jazmine smiles when the kiss ends.

Twenty minutes later, after calming herself, Jazmine says to Ray,

"Ray, help me understand all of this drama."

Ray looks pathetically ashamed.

"I don't even know how it got this far. My brother is obsessed with bringing Dylan's dad down. And now he's obsessed with her."

Jazmine asks,

"But why her? Dylan says he used to date her crazy-ass sister years ago."

Ray continues,

"Apparently that is why he's out to get her father. He forced them to break up. But he didn't stop there. He set him up, planted evidence linking him to a few murders in the city, and conveniently planted massive pounds of drugs in his room and car…enough to send him away for twenty years."

Jazmine listens intently.

"So now what? We can't let him hurt Dylan anymore."

Ray thinks hard.

"First I gotta figure out where they are."

Jazmine responds,

"I overheard them saying they were headed to Vegas for one of the biggest payoffs."

Ray looks confused as he tries to figure out what the payoff could be.

"Gotta probably bring my dad in…won't be hard—he despises her father just as much as Big Rob does."

Jazmine stops Ray's brainstorming session.

"I think it would be a better idea to bring Dylan's dad into this…She's who we need to find. Big Rob can go to hell."

Jazmine tries hard to convince Ray that Chief Jones needs to have the upper hand in this fight.

"Besides, her father probably knows every step Big Rob is making."

Ray hesitates in his decision to go to the chief of police in fear of the backlash he'll receive from his father and brother.

"I'll be disowned."

Ray struggles to make the choice, but is interrupted by the sound of familiar voices in the hallway. He looks at Jazmine in a panic.

"They're here for you. Let's go."

He grabs Jazmine by the arm and rushes her to Kennedy's room. He reveals a hidden passageway in her shoe closet. The two of them rush through the passageway, ending up in the basement. He looks out the back door, ensuring they are in the clear. They make a run for his blue Escalade. The sound of gunfire ricocheting from the top floor window leaves the two running and ducking. Ray peels out and instructs Jazmine to keep her head down through the unfriendly fire.

ৎৎ৹

Big Rob and his crew are at a warehouse in Las Vegas unloading FSW boxes off a trailer. His confidence shines through the deceit and schemes as he briefs the crew of their evening plans. Once Big Rob is assured his team of thugs is versed with positions and roles, he heads back to the Wynn to grab Dylan and Kennedy. He walks into the suite and finds the girls drinking and trying on clothes that he had sent over from a boutique. His suspicion of Dylan's transition to Demi has permanently faded, and the scene of drunken girls and laughter puts his mind at ease. Dylan cues her mischief behavior when she notices Big Rob staring at her. He strokes his goatee.

"A-ight, girls...let's get this party going. We gotta lot of potential clients."

Dylan's curiosity grows but she manages to keep it tucked tight as she plays her role of devious Demi.

"Just point me in the right direction and I'll sell whatever needs to be sold."

She giggles deviously. Kennedy's suspicion lessens, and she joins in the conversation.

"So what are we doing tonight?"

Big Rob looks at the pair of girls and smiles.

"Making me a rich man."

He walks over behind Dylan.

"Let me see you model."

He turns up the stereo, and Dylan starts walking the fake runway. She twirls, poses, and stands still. Her model call routine is

174

forcefully interrupted as a piercing pain shoots through her head. She holds the side of her head, screaming. Kennedy runs over to help her. Big Rob stares with concern.

"Demi...you aight? I need you to be your best tonight. Go lie down for a while."

Kennedy walks Dylan to the room and helps her lie down.

"What's wrong with you?"

Dylan's eyes begin to tear up but she heads them off with her quick wit.

"All that twirling with a stomach full of cocktails is what's wrong. Go get me a chicken bone to gnaw on." She laughs.

Kennedy returns a chuckle.

"All right, twin...I got you. Let me call room service."

Kennedy walks out of the room. Big Rob meets her in the hallway.

"Is she all right?"

Kennedy smiles.

"Damn, look who is really stuck on her. You got it bad, bro."

Big Rob speaks forcefully.

"Just answer the question."

Kennedy pauses for a moment.

"Yes, she just drank too much and is hungry."

Big Rob responds,

"Well, go get her some grub, and let's get this show on the road."

Two hours later, Dylan and Kennedy are standing in a ballroom full of a variety of men from all walks of life. Some are dressed in Italian suits, colored suits; some are dressed in jeans, polos, or white T-shirts and ball caps and Timberland boots; some are dressed in khakis and button-up collared shirts. They are all different, yet they possess one thing in common...their money could stretch across continents. Top-shelf liquors are poured and finger-sized treats are passed around to the men, self-proclaimed businessmen and entrepreneurs, who stand erect with pride as they are draped with elongated silhouettes of arm candy.

The lights dim and the black stage is illuminated with bright flashing lights, creating a runway. Big Rob, Dylan, and Kennedy are backstage getting prepped and dressed for the main event. Big Rob looks at Dylan and holds her hand,

"Demi...I need you to sell the shit out of all the shoes you see lined up alongside the ballroom. If you cater to those women...the men will buy, and I'll walk out of here a rich man."

Dylan smiles nervously and inhales slowly.

"Just point me to my runway."

As Dylan stands backstage waiting for her turn to walk the runway, she tries to piece together the connection between the FSW shoes and Big Rob becoming a rich man. A flashed memory unlocks a clue in her mind. She remembers the stench of cocaine and heroin being weighed, bagged, and packed in the identical FSW boxes. As she stands behind the curtain, the stage manager presses her back softly to motion her to walk out onstage. Dylan's head vibrates. Her eyes darken and her strut lands a distinct level of attitude with each step she takes. She introduces the fresh line of diva-inspired heels as she models a yellow suede pointed-toe knee-high boot. She kills the runway, and the audience of women applauds with enthusiasm and desire for a pair of their own. She sweats profusely, and she gives into the inevitable. Demi has awakened.

Big Rob stands behind stage, mesmerized by Demi's presence. When she returns backstage, he grabs her hand and whispers,

"I'm feeling real good. Let's make this official...we'll both be rich."

Chapter 20

EVERY PRINCESS NEEDS A HERO

The bullet-pierced Escalade pulls up in front of the Metropolitan Police Department. Jazmine steps out of the truck first. Her ripped pants and her bloodstained shirt catch the attention of many police officers walking past. The call of all on deck blazes through the walkie-talkies of the officers standing by, smoking their cancer sticks. Jazmine turns to motion Ray out of the truck.

"Come on…don't punk out."

Ray steps out of the SUV. He hesitates in stride as he walks slowly past the police officers. Sirens blaze through the air as fifty cruisers and unmarked police cars speed off en route to the call of distress. Jazmine and Ray walk into the police station and try to get past the front desk to see the chief. With every unsuccessful attempt, Ray slowly loses the nerve to disclose all the facts leading to Dylan's disappearance. Jazmine gets tired of everyone ignoring her requests, so she stands on the counter and yells at the top of her lungs,

"Excuse the fuck out of me…I am merely trying to help you muthafuckers do your job. We have information about the disappearance of Dylan…"

Before Jazmine can get the last word out, some rookie cop snatches her off the counter. Sergeant Foster is stepping off the elevator just as Jazmine is being thrown against the wall.

"Let her go. I heard the pretty lady say she has information."

The rookie releases his hold on her. Jazmine looks back at Ray...

"He's with me too."

Sergeant Foster motions for Ray to follow. Ray joins Jazmine and Sergeant Foster on the elevator. Sergeant Foster looks at Jazmine.

"You got a pretty bad cut on the back of your head. Did he do this to you?"

Jazmine grins slyly.

"Naw...the man you're hunting did this."

The trio steps off the elevator and heads toward Chief Jones's office. Sergeant Foster taps on the door to the office and awaits Chief Jones's invitation to enter.

Sergeant Foster walks in first.

"Chief...these two young people..."

Chief Jones interrupts. I know who this is. This is Dylan's best friend and her punk of a boyfriend, Raymond Kendrick."

Sergeant Foster draws his gun.

"Easy, son...he's harmless. The deviant is the one with my baby girl. This one here is a little pussy."

Chief Jones holds his arms open for Jazmine.

"Sweetheart, what happened to you?"

They snuck up on us in the club, kidnapped us, and they left me for dead. They took her, Mr. Jones. We gotta get her back."

"How was she when you last saw her?"

"She was still Dylan. But I don't know how long that will last."

Chief Jones and Sergeant Foster separate Jazmine and Ray. Sergeant Foster leads Ray to an interrogation room to force any and all information from him. Jazmine is escorted to the hospital for treatment of her wounds and a potential concussion.

∞

At the Wynn Resort & Casino, Big Rob's excitement over his successful night spills over into the morning light. He wakes Demi with an influx of climaxes and breakfast. The morning bond and radiant pillow talk is interrupted by Big Rob's ringing cell phone. Big Rob leaves Demi lying in their puddle of love. She rolls over, turns on the television, and waits for Big Rob to return.

Big Rob enters the living room of the suite and sits on the couch with his hand in his pants. He tries to sit through the screaming, psychotic voice on the other end of the phone that is trying to reason with him.

"It was supposed to be you and me forever. Do you remember that? I've lost everything because of you. I thought you loved me. Couldn't live without me. That is supposed to be me running and hiding out with you. Jumping fences and dodging bullets. Why do you keep leaving me?"

Big Rob quickly loses interest.

"Look, Janay. You're a cop. I'm a bad boy for life. It will never work."

Janay screams hysterically.

"I'm no longer a police officer. I've been fired. So I'm all yours."

Empathetic toward Janay's hysteria, Big Rob gives her an ultimatum.

179

"Prove to me you can be trusted. Kill your father. And then you can join the family."

Janay pauses.

"Done. He's dead to me anyway."

Big Rob's third leg grows erect from her loyalty.

"All right then. Call me when it's done. I'll verify—then I'll send for you."

Before Big Rob hangs up the phone, he hears Janay's pitiful voice bellow out,

"Rob, I love you. I always have."

He ends the call without responding. He stands up and walks back in the room with Demi. His mountain peak is pushing high through his sweatpants. He jumps back into bed and aggressively reveals how excited he is to be in between the sheets with her.

Chief Jones leaves the station and heads home to get ready for Dylan's search and rescue. Ray's honest confession of his brother and father's activities gives Chief Jones the upper hand. He makes a call to Dr. Roberts. As soon as she agrees to meet with him, he heads over to her office. Chief Jones walks into her practice. Dr. Roberts sits behind her desk typing on the computer. She stands to shake Chief Jones's hand.

"Nice to see you. How is everything going? How's Dylan?"

Chief Jones sighs.

"Not good. I need your help."

Dr. Roberts walks over to the door and closes it to give the two of them some privacy. She returns to her desk and grabs her pad and pen. Chief Jones sits down. He speaks cautiously as he hands her a brown envelope.

Chief Jones fills Dr. Roberts in on Dylan's current situation. Dr. Roberts opens her drawer, pulls out a prescription pad and quickly writes a dosage, followed by detailed instructions. She rips the slip off the pad and secures it on the inside of a manila folder. She places the manila folder inside a large white envelope and hands both the envelope and a pill bottle to Chief Jones. She smiles warmly.

"This should help get her back to her normal levels. But make sure she takes them daily."

Chief Jones graciously smiles and thanks her.

"Lynette…I mean, Dr. Roberts, thank you. This will save my baby girl's life…especially if something was to happen to me."

Chief Jones exits her office and heads home.

A half hour later, he enters the threshold of his home. He calls out to Carmen. The plague of silence and an aroma-free house triggers Chief Jones's radar. He appreciates the smoke-free rooms and calmness. He heads to his home office on the side of the main house. Chief Jones sits at his desk and sifts through the various notes he's collected. He circles the word, *Las Vegas* written on the notepad. He drags out a box from under his desk and unlocks it. The top of the wooden box has the word, *Jamaica,* and the front has *Home Sweet Home* carved into the wood. He pulls out a sausage-link-sized ganja roll. He sniffs it briefly and grips the top edge with his lips. Chief Jones flicks the metal hinges to the wooden carved lighter. As soon as the flame blazes through the tip of the chocolate roll, he licks his lips in anticipation of the long-awaited drag. It's interrupted by the ringing sound of his cell phone. He leans forward in the chair and takes a deep breath and clears the thick phlegm out of his throat before speaking.

"Chief Jones here. Speak and speak fast."

He pauses.

"Hello."

The voice on the other end is whispering.

"Daddy. Hello, Daddy. It's me. I can't talk long. I just wanted to tell you I'm OK."

Chief Jones stands up on his feet.

"Baby girl, I know you're in Vegas...but I need you to tell me where."

Dylan cries through the phone in panic.

"Daddy, I don't have long. I have to hurry. She'll be back. I just want to tell you...

Dylan screams out hysterically.

"My head hurts so bad. I don't have much time. She's coming back. I'm at the..."

She cries out in agony.

"I just wanted to protect you. I don't want you to die."

She screams in distress again.

"Take care of you and Mommy. I love you. Don't worry about me."

The phone goes dead. Chief Jones starts dialing numbers on his desk phone, inputting numbers incorrectly. His eyes are red and his nostrils flare uncontrollably. The phone rings on the other end. An operator answers.

"Yes, this is Chief Jones. I need a triangular trace on this number: two-four-zero three-three-four three-eight-one-eight. I'm at home in my office. I need the location...yesterday. Now transfer me to Sergeant Foster."

While waiting for Sergeant Foster to answer the phone, Chief Jones places the call on speaker. He starts rummaging through his closet and opens up the wall safe. He reveals a massive line of artillery. He pulls out a book in his desk and searches for the name of one of his oldest and dearest friends. He then calls in a favor with the chief of police in Las Vegas. He places the white envelope he received from Dr. Roberts inside his desk drawer and locks it.

‿

A tall, slender, handsome silhouette stands in front of the window rubbing his goatee with his left hand while he uses his right hand to rub the warm brunette tresses on top of the oval-shaped head of the woman whose lips are spit-shining the tip of his penis. The right hand halts the bouncing head in motion to cease but not release. The slender male backs up slowly, gliding the lock-jawed woman to follow his path to the ringing desk phone. He uses his left hand to turn on the lamp to his desk to get clear visibility of the phone number on the LCD screen. He grabs the receiver and holds the bouncing bobblehead, motioning for permission to continue. He speaks slowly through his enjoyment.

"Sergeant Foster...mmm, I mean, hi, Chief Jones."

Chief Jones begins talking.

"A location is being gathered. Assemble your team. We need to get in and out. No questions, only results. Muster the troops for debriefing in an hour."

Sergeant Foster fails to get one "kiss ass" word in before the chief hangs up the phone. He pulls the bobbing head up to stand eye to eye with him. He looks at her smeared mascara and says rudely,

"That's enough, lock jaw. I'll redeem my payout. My winning streak is unbelievable."

The woman wipes her mouth and replaces her breast inside her bra. She buttons her shirt and swirls her hair into a bun. She zips her thigh-high boots while smiling at Sergeant Foster. She says sharply,

"We can certainly wager a little more than a game of spades next time...perhaps somewhere else more comfortable than your office."

Sergeant Foster smiles while zipping up his pants. He waves her out of his office and responds deviously,

"If only you were a bit more polished. These walls are where you belong."

༄

Sergeant Foster meets up with Chief Jones at their usual meeting place, the Garage, a bar and grill where Chief Jones goes for his daily beer and buffalo chicken wings.

Sergeant Foster walks in with his charismatic strut. He sifts his moist third leg into a comfortable position as he passes by beautiful women sitting in groups at the bar. He approaches the booth where Chief Jones is dressed in all black with a black hat. The chief is talking to two men—an older man dressed in all black and a younger man dressed in a business suit.

As soon as Sergeant Foster walks close, Chief Jones introduces the pair to Sergeant Foster.

"Eric, this is one of my dearest and oldest friends, Lucky. He's the godfather of my girls and the godfather of the underground."

Sergeant Foster shakes Lucky's hand.

Chief Jones continues the introductions.

"...and this here to my left is another good man, Kenneth Smith. I call him my future son-in-law."

Sergeant Foster has a smug look but follows suit and shakes Kenneth's hand. Chief Jones continues,

"Lucky, Kenneth, this is the son I never had...Sgt. Eric Foster."

Sergeant Foster stands proudly at the introduction. He sits down and grins.

"It's an honor. Any friends of the chief are surely friends of mine."

The four men discuss strategy and leave the Garage at midnight to meet their teams for deployment. Chief Jones hands a set of keys to Kenneth and hugs him briefly before Kenneth departs the team. Lucky calls in a favor and has a private jet fueled and ready to go to transport the team of enraged off-duty police officers to sin city.

Back at the Joneses' estate, Carmen returns home from a secretive visit with an old friend. She notices no one is home. She calls her husband on the phone to find out if he's gotten any closer to finding Dylan. He answers just before the plane takes off. While Carmen is talking to Jonathan, Janay walks through the door. She overhears her mother talking to her father. She sneaks back out the door after discovering her father is en route to save his lil' princess.

Janay jumps back in her car and dials Big Rob. After several rings, Big Rob answers the phone. She can hardly hear him through the spinning wheels and slot machines in the casino. Big Rob answers, and Janay sings like a chorus.

"Rob, wanted to give you heads up…my father is on his way to Vegas.

"I thought you were taking care of that problem. He was supposed to be deleted yesterday. What the fuck do you want with me?"

Janay tries to talk in between his rants.

Big Rob continues spewing.

"So what—he's on his way. He has no jurisdiction. He can bring it…I'm gonna light that ass up."

Janay stumbles through her words.

"Wait. I'm gonna keep my promise. I got it. I just wanted to…"

Before she can finish, she hears a woman in the background talking to Big Rob.

"Mr. Kendrick, these are all the wedding packages we have available."

Janay starts screaming through the phone, trying to get Big Rob's attention. She grows excited.

"Rob, hello…Rob. Are you planning our wedding?"

Big Rob catches the tail end of her question.

"Bitch, you tripping. Get off my phone."

Big Rob hangs up on her. Janay is hysterical. She starts screaming and crying. She steps outside her car and pops the trunk open. She pulls a bag out, unzips it, and opens it to look through the contents. She picks up Dylan's police academy application, a CD, and an envelope of pictures. She heads down to the twenty-four-hour post office. She looks at the CD once more, ensuring the text written on the label is clear. It reads, West Virginia Murder—Evidence. She seals the envelope of photos and writes on the front, clearly and concisely. She glances over the typed letter she created. She laughs as she reads the words.

Is this the type of recruit you're seeking to hire? You should spend more time digging up the past of the many recruits storming through your doors. Perhaps this could be the first assignment of your graduates…bringing justice to a city that protects common criminals like her.

Janay places the letter, the CD, the application, and the envelope full of pictures into a larger express mail envelope. She seals it tight and requests overnight delivery to the Metropolitan Police Academy.

Janay hops in her car and heads down North Capitol Street, headed toward I-395. Twenty minutes later, she's pulling onto the ramp for airport departures and drives into the garage marked long-term parking. She looks at her watch and programs it for 6:00 p.m. to synchronize with Las Vegas time.

Chapter 21

THOSE IN THE DARK...

BE ENLIGHTENED

At 6:30 p.m., the team of off-duty renegade police land at the private hanger of the Las Vegas airport. They stand in a huddle of support as they pray silently for a quick deployment and safe return. The Las Vegas police chief stands at the bottom of the stairs of the plane as the team, dressed in all black, exits. Chief Jonathan Jones is the last to exit. As soon as he walks up to the patiently waiting police chief, they shake hands, and the city of Las Vegas welcomes them.

The deployed team is driven to the Las Vegas police station where the whole team is greeted with hot food and beverages. Chief Jones and the police chief stand outside the room where everyone else feasts, and they strategize with each other about the easiest way to get into the Wynn Resort & Casino without disrupting everyone or putting any lives at risk.

Chief Jones stands with his hands in his pockets, as the police chief briefs him,

"I don't know how many of his guys are in there, but I hear he has a small army."

Chief Jones stands tall in preparation for moving his troops out to the battlefield. He grunts and clears his throat.

"As I stated before, I have one focus. She's precious to me. Even if things go sour, our success will be her freedom."

The two chiefs shake hands. Two hours later, the Vegas chief of police receives a call from a security detail inside of the Wynn Hotel, confirming the location of Big Rob and his crew. The two chiefs brief the Vegas and Metropolitan police teams on the strategy.

Chief Jones announces,

"In exactly two hours, all men will be in position. We get in and get out. We bring the precious cargo back here for deployment."

At 9:45 p.m., eight teams are loaded into black, unmarked cargo trucks. Four teams enter the back of the Wynn Resort & Casino. The building manager clears the floors and hallways on and in between the targeted wedding chapel. The next four teams are deployed to the front of the hotel. Guests and staff are quickly herded away, off the floor.

The wedding chapel is dimly lit with white strings of crystal draped from the ceiling. Kennedy stands at the front of the chapel beside Big Rob, as they wait for Demi to walk down the aisle. The teams of armed cops are outlined across the front, back, and side perimeters of the chapel. Demi walks down in a white cocktail dress, wearing a pair of white pointed pumps with a white bow on the back. She smiles as she gracefully walks down the aisle. She approaches Big Rob and Kennedy. She hugs Kennedy and places her arm inside Big Rob's left arm.

The officiator joins the couple. He begins reciting the themed Romeo and Juliet vows chosen by the couple. Big Rob turns to Demi and professes his undying love for her. Demi smiles and nervously laughs when it's her turn. She reads the written words given to her by the wedding planner. She turns to Big Rob and professes her attraction for his continuous adventure. The officiator speaks seriously to the couple, and he asks Big Rob if he takes Demi's hand in marriage. Big Rob smiles before responding,

"I never thought I would be saying this...but I do."

The officiator turns to Demi, and he asks her if she accepts Big Rob's hand in marriage. As soon as Demi fixes her lips to respond, the doors to the chapel are thrust open and the chapel is swarming with armed men. Demi is stunned and stands frozen. Chief Jones appears from behind the army of cops. He frantically yells,

"Dylan, wait."

Demi chuckles.

"Sir, continue...and hurry."

The officiator asks Demi the question again.

"Do you take his hand in marriage?"

Demi is interrupted once again. She stomps her feet and turns to face Chief Jones.

"Chief, you're just in time. I's gettin' married...you see, Dylan is gone. She's checked out, and this is what I want."

Chief Jones makes his way to the front of the chapel, yelling.

"You can't...you won't. Over my dead body."

Big Rob starts laughing out loud and says,

"That can be arranged."

Chief Jones and Big Rob stare at each other from a distance. Big Rob's goons stand up from the pews. They all begin reaching for their guns.

Chief Jones continues,

"Dylan...sweetheart. You're coming with me. This criminal is going to be taken into custody."

Demi sighs with frustration.

"Let me finish. I...I do."

As soon as Demi bellows those words, Chief Jones runs toward her screaming,

"No…you can't. He's not who you think. He's…"

Shots ring out from behind a closed door, sending broken glass and wood chips projecting through the air. Chief Jones's forehead is a bull's-eye target for the pointed tip of the brass-covered bullet encased with an explosion of powder, ripping the skeletal core of Chief Jones's frontal lobe. Chaos breaks out as all the cops start shooting up Big Rob's goons. Demi is swooped off her feet and rushed through the back doors. She's thrown in the back of an SUV and taken out of harm's way. The blazing sound of police and ambulance sirens echoes through the city in search of the gunmen. Big Rob is taken away in handcuffs. Kennedy is placed on a gurney with non-life-threatening injuries.

Sergeant Foster rides in the front passenger seat as the driver speeds to the Las Vegas airport. He stirs a white mixture of powder into the opening of a brand new bottle of Pepsi. He closes the pill bottle that has *Dylan Jones* written on its label. He turns to wake Demi out of her slumber and hands her the Pepsi. She sits upright and holds her head in disbelief. She starts chanting rhythmically,

"He's dead. The chief is dead, he's dead."

She keeps repeating the phrase over and over in between sips of Pepsi. The two step on the plane at the private hanger at the Las Vegas airport. Sergeant Foster sits her down and makes sure she's comfortable. Demi looks at Sergeant Foster with sadness.

"Why is the chief dead?"

Sergeant Foster is speechless. Demi lays her head back and sleeps for the duration of the flight.

In the nation's capital, Carmen receives a phone call from the police chief of Las Vegas. He delivers the bad news to Carmen as she sits at her computer playing Texas Hold'em.

She hangs up the phone. Then she dials a number. When the person on the other end of the phone picks up, Carmen says slowly,

"Did you do this? Did you have my husband killed?"

She immediately breaks down before the individual can answer. She hangs up sobbing and smoking, crying out loud,

"My husband, the hero...he's dead, No, he can't be dead. He's my hero."

❧

On January 17, relatives from across the island of Jamaica and the states of Philadelphia, New York, and New Jersey gather together to pay tribute to the life of Chief Jonathan Jones. Demi's traumatic experience forces a loss of control over Dylan. Sergeant Foster explains to Dylan a few days after their return from Vegas that Chief Jones managed to hand him her medicine the night of his death in an attempt to save her.

Dylan's awakening brings her a new strength that she hadn't yet discovered. The morning of Chief Jones's funeral, Dylan stands in the center of her walk-in closet, surrounded by stacked shelves on her closet wall, full of various styles of shoes. She takes a quick glance at the many pairs of shoes that brought her countless hours of promiscuity, sensual, daredevil, yet youthful experiences. She drops her head as she remembers her lustful, yet shameful, episodes of fornicating sessions in the stairways of her band rehearsals with Ray. She shakes her head shamefully, speaking out loud to herself,

"I did anything for shoes. Look what it got me."

Her mind begins to play tricks internally. She hears laughter in her mind. She walks close to a red leather stiletto peeptoe sandal shelved above her short stature. She leans in as she hears the chattering of many voices laughing. Dylan glimpses at a pair of classic black leather pointed-toe pumps. Her eyes begin to water as she remembers the day her father handed her a red shoebox filled with the classic pumps. It was the morning of her high school graduation. Dylan reaches inside one of the shoes and pulls out a small square card. Tears flow heavily from her eyes as she reads the card.

To my princess…Only a classy girl can wear a classy pair. Be the best you are destined to become. Happy graduation. Love, Dad.

She sobs for minutes, and then she forces herself to gather her composure. Dylan glances at her funeral attire. She holds back the tears as she slips into a black leather skirt, black blouse, and a black cardigan. She exits the closet and walks into her bathroom, opens the medicine cabinet, and grabs her prescription bottle. She reads the label, noticing she doesn't have any refills left and makes a mental note that she needs to make an appointment with Dr. Roberts. As Dylan pops the pill, landing it in the back of her mouth, she gulps a handful of water from the faucet and throws her head back to swallow her mental issues away. She faces the mirror and smiles at her newly gained strength, but she fears the agonizing pain her father's death would welcome old friends and possibly new ones.

Two hours later, she stands proudly at the funeral service and delivers a eulogy that brings every woman and man to tears. After the funeral service, Dylan stays behind while everyone drives away from the cemetery. She lies down beside the fresh grave that encases her father's casket. She talks and sings to her father, thanking him for his courage in order to deliver her freedom.

A pair of footsteps startles Dylan as she sobs in celebration of her father's death. A figure with a deranged pair of eyes stares at her and brandishes a gun. Dylan jumps up.

"Janay. Where the fuck you been? Why weren't you at Daddy's funeral?"

Janay starts laughing and talking to herself. She mumbles deranged thoughts and blames Dylan for her failures. She starts screaming at Dylan,

"He was mine. He always was. You were the pitiful charity case. He was mine. He was never yours...all mine."

Dylan starts yelling at Janay,

"Get away from my father's grave, you disrespectful disappointment."

Janay stands erect with piercing eyes. She charges Dylan and pushes her into the hole on top of their father's casket, knocking Dylan out of her shoes. Janay aims her gun directly at her. Shots ring through the air. A hush cascades across the trees and grass.

A blanket of rain gushes over the grave, spilling puddles inside the black stiletto pumps, leaving imprints of mud and mayhem...and the cemetery grows dark.

EPILOGUE

FALL 2012

BACK WOODS AND FOLIAGE

The sun-kissed mountains pump off steam as the humidity decreases. The calmness of the season sparks renewal in the community of St. Ann's Parish. A petite, curvy woman stands on the cobblestone driveway in black stretch jeans and a white tank top that rises over her protruding belly. Her ashy ankles and toes outline a pair of dusty flip-flops. The blazing sunrays warm her glowing cheeks as her asymmetric hair strands stick to her sweaty chin and neck. She stands with confidence, persuading the bugs to fly away. The tunes of reggae music seep through the windows of the homestead, and elders sit on the porch and rock to the bass of the music. The young woman joins the group of elders on the porch. She sits down and grabs her guitar. Her long thumbs brush the strings on the guitar, vibrating beats of melodic tunes behind the reggae music. She bellows out passionate chords, mimicking her earlier rock sessions with the Flaming Rejects.

His love is the light and his gift was my life,
He loved me, yes he did.
His love is so strong, and his legend lives on.

When the song ends, the woman leans in close to her elders, who are chewing on sugarcane and sipping from cans of Red Stripe. She rubs her belly while pulling her tank top over the protruding bump. She smiles at her aging great-grandmother and speaks hoarsely.

"Great-grand…Mi want to hear more riddles to teach mi little one about mi grand's early life."

The wrinkled great-grandmother leans close to her great-granddaughter. She begins chanting spiritual hymns to raise the spirit of her son. She calls out,

"Mi hope ya listening. Oh, Jonathan, come listen."

The young woman rocks back and forth and closes her eyes as she visualizes happy times with the man she once called Daddy.

Dear Reader,

I hope you enjoyed *If These Shoes Could Talk: The Awakening*. Dylan Jones is a unique character that crawled out of my bucket of observations. She's very special to me, and I have many plans for her in the future. I hope as you read through all the pages, you have either grown to like Dylan or love her alter ego, Demi. Whichever you like or dislike, I hope I've intrigued your mind.

As I prepare the next part of this book series, *If These Shoes Could Talk: The Rebellion*…get to know Dylan Jones more intimately. Socially connect with Dylan:

Facebook: https://www.facebook.com/BeingDylanJones
Twitter: https://twitter.com/BeingDylanJones
Tumblr: http://beingdylanjones.tumblr.com/

Thank You for Your Support!

-Jahzara, the Savvy Diva

www.ingramcontent.com/pod-product-compliance
Lightning Source LLC
Chambersburg PA
CBHW070124260626
47160CB00004B/1605